SEVEN O'CLOCK STORIES

ROBERT GORDON ANDERSON

1st WORLD
LIBRARY
Literary Society

Seven O'Clock Stories

Robert Gordon Anderson

© 1st World Library – Literary Society, 2004
PO Box 2211
Fairfield, IA 52556
www.1stworldlibrary.org
First Edition

LCCN: 2004195349

Softcover ISBN: 1-4218-0183-3
Hardcover ISBN: 1-4218-0083-7
eBook ISBN: 1-4218-0283-X

Purchase *"Seven O'Clock Stories"*
as a traditional bound book at:
www.1stWorldLibrary.org/purchase.asp?ISBN=1-4218-0183-3

Seven O'Clock Stories
contributed by Tim, Ed & Rodney
in support of
1st World Library Literary Society

TO JEAN AND MALCOLM

TO WHOM THESE STORIES WERE FIRST TOLD

CONTENTS

THE THREE HAPPY CHILDREN 7

THE PLAYMATES OF THE THREE HAPPY
CHILDREN.. 10

NOISY FOLKS 14

JUST BEFORE SUPPER 18

THE TOYMAN................................... 22

THE WILLOW WHISTLE 27

MR. SCARECROW 31

THE PRETTIEST FAIRY STORY IN THE WORLD 38

ANOTHER TRUE FAIRY STORY........................ 45

THE HAPPY ENDING OF THE ORIOLE'S STORY........... 52

MOTHER HEN AND ROBBER HAWK 59

ABOUT DUCKIE THE STEPCHILD AND
THE LITTLE SHIP 67

THE TALL ENEMY 80

THE SLEIGH AND THE TINY REINDEER........................ 89

JACK FROST AND THE MAN-IN-THE-MOON 97

SLOSHIN' 110

THE CIRCUS COMES TO TOWN 121

THE JOLLY CLOWN 131

WIENERWURST'S BRAVE BATTLE 144

THE LIONS OF THE NORTH WIND 152

FIRST NIGHT

THE THREE HAPPY CHILDREN

Not once upon a time but just now, in a white house by the side of a road, live three happy children.

Their mother and father gave them very odd names, for two old uncles and one aunt, which pleased the old people very much. Their names are all written in the big family Bible, - Jehosophat Green, Marmaduke Green, and Hepzebiah Green.

Jehosophat is just seven years old. His birthday comes on Thanksgiving Day this year. It does not come on Thanksgiving Day every year, of course. See if you can guess why.

Marmaduke is five, "going on six," he always says. Little Hepzebiah, who toddles after her brothers, tells everyone who comes to visit that she is "half-past three." She heard her brother say this once and she imitates all he does and says. Perhaps that is why her father calls her a "little monkey."

These happy children all live in the country. They do not know much about elevated trains and subways and automobiles and moving pictures but they do know a great deal about flowers and birds and chestnuts and picnics and lots of things which you would like too, if you lived in the country.

Each place you see has its advantages. All good is not found in the country, nor all in the city. If we keep both eyes open we will see lots of enjoyable and beautiful things wherever we are.

The house in which Jehosophat and Marmaduke and Hepzebiah live is large. It has many rooms to sleep in and eat in and play in. It is painted white and has wide windows with green blinds.

Around the house are large trees. The branches seem to pat the house lovingly and to protect the children when the sun is too hot or the rain comes down too fast.

They are fine for swings and bird-houses, these trees, and some throw down acorns and others cones and soft pine needles for the children to play with.

Behind the house and gardens are red barns, chicken yards - and oh lots of animals, - the three dogs, Rover, Brownie, and little yellow Wienerwurst and all the rest. You will come to know them later. Each has his funny ways and queer tricks just like people. Around the house are fields with growing plants and oh - we almost forgot the pond where Jehosophat and his brother sail boats.

Mother, that is Mrs. Green, is not too thin nor yet too plump. She is just what a mother ought to be, with kind, shining eyes, and soft cheeks. She is always cooking things or doing things for Jehosophat and Marmaduke and little Hepzebiah.

Robert Gordon Anderson

Father - the neighbours call him Neighbour Green - is very strong. He can lift big weights and manage bad horses. He can do lots of work and yet somehow he finds time to do things for the children too.

His eyes are blue, while mother's are brown. When he laughs, Marmaduke thinks it sounds like the church-bells on Sunday. Once he had a moustache but that went when mother said he would look younger without it. Now sometimes, when he works hard, he does not have time to shave every day. On Sunday mornings Hepzebiah loves to watch him take the brush and cup. The cup has flowers painted on it. When he turns the brush in the cup it makes something like whipped cream, or the top of mother's lemon pies.

And after he takes it off with the razor his face is red and shiny and smooth. Hepzebiah always likes to kiss her father, but she likes to kiss him best on Sunday mornings.

Tonight you have met all the family so we must stop for the clock says "after seven." Tomorrow we will meet all the animals and they are really part of the family too.

SECOND NIGHT

THE PLAYMATES OF THE
THREE HAPPY CHILDREN

The three happy children have many playmates, who live in the barnyard. Some have four feet and some only two, but *these* have two wings besides to make up for the missing feet.

Jehosophat, Marmaduke, and Hepzebiah like the dogs best. And just as there are three children so there are three dogs. Let's shake hands with them, one by one.

The great big dog is named Rover, the middle-sized one Brownie, and the little yellow curly one Wienerwurst.

A wise fellow is Rover. From a cold country called Newfoundland his great grandfather came. And he seems to think life is a very serious matter. His coat is black with snow-white patches. His hair curls a little. It feels very soft when you lay your head against it.

He doesn't play as much as the other two doggies. But once when Hepzebiah fell in the pond after her doll, Rover swam in and caught her dress in his mouth and brought her to shore. Not long after that Mr. Green gave him a new shiny collar.

Brownie is a terrier and is coloured like his name. He is a frisky dog and often chases the horses and buggies that go up and down the road in front of the house. Sometimes the drivers lash at him with their long whips but he is too quick for them and scampers out of their reach.

The funniest doggie in all the world is little yellow Wienerwurst. He is even more full of mischief than Brownie and loves to run after all the other animals in the barnyard.

When the pigeons fly down from their little house on the top of the barn to take an afternoon walk and perhaps pick up a few extra grains of corn, this little yellow doggie spoils all their fun. He soon sends them flying back to their house on the roof, where they chatter and coo in great excitement. But they do not lose their tempers like "Mr. Stuckup," the turkey, or old "Miss Crosspatch," the guinea-hen with the ugly voice.

Once little Wienerwurst caught a pretty pigeon by its tail and bit it. Then Mr. Green took him over his knee, just as he did Jehosophat when he threw a stone at the window, and spanked little Wienerwurst.

Each dog has a house. One is big, one middle-sized, and one small, and each has a door to fit the doggie who lives there. Their houses are called kennels, and they are something like the pigeon's home way up on the roof.

The pigeons are very pretty, grey and white and pink coloured. When the sun shines brightly their necks shine too, like the rainbow silk dress which Mrs. Green wears whenever there is a wedding.

One pair of the pigeons sit a great deal of the time on the ridge-pole of the barn and swell out their chests like proud, fat policemen. Farmer Green calls them pouter pigeons.

They do not have harsh voices like the guinea-hen or the old black crows which steal the corn from the field when Mr. Scarecrow gets tired and goes to sleep. (We will introduce you to Mr. Scarecrow some evening very soon.) But the voices of the pigeons are soft and low like mother's, especially when Hepzebiah is sick and she sings her to sleep.

They will not have much to do with the chickens, these pigeons. Perhaps they are like the people who live on the top floor of tall city houses and do not go down often to talk with the people in the streets.

What a lot of chickens Farmer Green has! Almost two hundred, if they would ever stay still long enough for Jehosophat to count them. They are called White Wyandottes and they are very white and plump, with combs as red as geraniums.

You know there are many kinds of chickens just as there are many kinds of people, English, French, and Americans. Rhode Island Reds, Plymouth Rocks, Cochins, and Leghorns are some of the chicken family names, but Jehosophat's father does not believe in mixing families, he says, so only the White Wyandottes live on the Green farm.

Jehosophat and Marmaduke love the big rooster best. The red comb on the top of his head has teeth like a carpenter's saw, and is so large it will not stand up straight. His white tail curves beautifully like the plumes on the hats of the circus ladies. When he throws back his head, puffs out his throat, and calls to the Sun, he is indeed a wonderful creature.

The little chicks are the ones Hepzebiah loves best. She can hold them in her two hands like little soft yellow balls or the powder puffs which Nurse uses on new little babies. The little chicks have such tiny voices, crying "cheep, cheep, cheep," almost the way the crickets do all through the night.

The chickens have cousins who - but there goes the clock - so that is tomorrow night's story.

THIRD NIGHT

NOISY FOLKS

Do you remember what we were telling about last night when that little tongue told us to stop? The little tongue in the Clock-with-the-Wise-Face on the mantel?

Oh yes, the first cousins of the chickens who lived in the yard of the three happy children.

Their first cousins are called ducks. Most of them are white but a few are black. Their coats are very smooth, and the skin under them sends out little drops of oil like drops of perspiration. This keeps the water and the rain from wetting the ducks through and through. You have heard people say sometimes: "The way water runs off a duck's back." Well, now you know the reason why.

In rainy weather Hepzebiah wears a blue waterproof with a little hood but the ducks do not need anything like that. Their everyday coats of white and black are just as good. If the White Wyandottes cannot get under the chicken coop or the barn quick enough when it rains, their feathers are all mussed up but the ducks seem always dressed in their best.

Robert Gordon Anderson

Their bills are different from their relatives'. They are not short and pointed like the chicken's but broad and long.

And they have what are called web feet. Between the toes are pieces of skin, thick and tough like canvas. These web feet are like small oars or paddles. With them they can push against the water of the pond and swim quite fast.

The ducks are very fond of the pond but their cousins think it a dreadful place.

"Cluck, cluck," say the White Wyandottes, "what a foolish way of spending your time, sailing on the water when there are fat, brown worms to dig for in the nice earth!"

You see animals, like people, like different things. The world wouldn't be half so interesting if we all liked the *same* things, would it?

The other night Jehosophat felt very foolish when he came in to supper. His mother looked behind his ears and said: "Why you are just as afraid of the water as the chickens."

Did you ever hear of such a thing!

Now the chickens have *second* cousins too. Their second cousins are the white geese.

They live on the other side of the tall fence that looks as if it were made of crocheted wire. Sometimes Jehosophat's father opens the gate in the fence and lets the geese wander down to the pond. A silly way they have of stretching out their long white necks and crying, "Hiss, hiss!" This frightens Hepzebiah who always runs away. Then the geese waddle along in single file, that is one by one, like fat old ladies crossing a muddy street on their way to sewing society.

Jehosophat says that the chickens have third cousins too, - the swans. There they are, way out on the pond, sailing along like white ships. Their necks are very long and snowy white and they bend in such a pretty way. And their soft white wings look something like the wings of the angels on the Christmas cards.

Jehosophat, Marmaduke, and Hepzebiah do not like one barnyard neighbour very much. It is the guinea-hen. She has a grey body, plump as a sack of meal, with little white speckles, a funny neck and such a small head with a tuft on top. She screeches horribly and Marmaduke calls her "Miss Crosspatch."

But the turkey with his proud walk is just funny. And yet Farmer Green says he hasn't any sense of humour. Ask *your* father how that can be if he is funny.

"Mr. Stuckup" the children call the turkey. He walks along slowly, swinging from side to side. His feathers are brownish-black or bronze, and his tail often spreads out like a fan. He has the funniest nose. It is red and soft and long and flops over his bill on his chest.

He calls "gobble, gobble, gobble," all the time, yet he does not gobble as much as the busy White Wyan-dottes all around him who are forever looking for kernels of corn or worms or bugs.

But who is this magnificent creature coming along

over the lawn under the cherry-tree? Uncle Roger, who sails around the world in a great ship with white sails, gave him to the children. He brought him from a land very far across the seas.

He is the peacock and is all green and gold and blue. On his head is a little crown of feathers. His tail, too, can spread out like a fan the way "Mr. Stuckup's," the turkey's, does. But it is ever so much more beautiful. It is green and has hundreds of blue eyes in it. The three children call him the "Party Bird" for he is always so dressed up, but their father says he is "a bit of a snob." He means that he is vain and will not have much to do with his plainer neighbours of the barnyard -

"One, two, three, four, five, six, seven." There goes the clock again.

Tomorrow night, if you are good all day, we will tell you about the rest of the barnyard friends of the three happy children. Then the next night, about the exciting things that happened to them.

Good-night! Sweet Dreams!

FOURTH NIGHT

JUST BEFORE SUPPER

In the afternoon the sun grows tired of his hot walk across the sky. Beyond the Green farm are the blue hills behind which he sleeps each night.

When he is almost there the three happy children go down to the barn to watch their four-footed friends come home.

Sometimes Frank, the hired man who helps Farmer Green, is late and does not go for the cows. All day long they have been in pasture. Sometimes they eat the grass and pink clover. Sometimes they wade in the little brook which flows there. But when it grows late, even if Frank does not come, they know it is supper time and leave the pasture.

When they reach the barnyard fence they stand outside calling to be let in. Then Frank comes and lets down the bars. They walk into the yard and through the doors into the big red barn.

There are ten cows but Jehosophat, Marmaduke, and Hepzebiah love four of them better than the rest. Their names are "Primrose," "Daisy," "Buttercup," and "Black-eyed Susan."

Now just as there are different kinds of chickens so there are several kinds of cows - Guernseys, Jerseys, Alderneys, and Holsteins.

"Primrose," "Daisy," and "Buttercup" are Jerseys and are a pretty brown. "Black-eyed Susan" belongs to the Holsteins and is black and white. "Black-eyed Susan" gives more milk than her companions but their milk has richer cream.

Each cow has a stall to sleep in. In front of each is a box or manger. Frank climbs up the tall ladder to the loft, which is the second story of the barn, and throws down the hay. Then he takes his sharp pitchfork and tosses a lot of hay in each manger. You would never think cows could eat so much. One box of shredded-wheat would do for all the Green family and visitors too, but "Primrose" and "Daisy" and all the rest each eat enough hay to fill many shredded-wheat boxes.

Jehosophat, Marmaduke, and Hepzebiah love to stand in the doorway of the barn and smell the hay as the cows chew it. It is very sweet smelling.

They do not go too near the stalls, for while the cows are eating their supper, they switch their tails to keep off the flies. Once "Black-eyed Susan" switched her tail across Marmaduke's face. It felt like a whip and he ran away crying. But "Susan" didn't mean it for she is a very gentle cow.

And once Jehosophat came too near old "Crumplety Horn," the white cow with the twisted horn. She kicked at Jehosophat and over went the pail of milk which his father had almost full.

The children like to see their father and Frank sit on their three-legged stools in the stalls and milk the cows. The milk spurts into the pails and it sounds very pleasant.

The milk is very warm when it comes from the cows so Farmer Green puts it in great cans as tall as Jehosophat. Then he carries the cans to the springhouse where it is cool, and leaves them overnight by the well. The children will drink some of it in the morning. Tonight they will drink *this morning's* milk, which is cool now.

About the time the cows come home the horses come back too.

First comes "Hal" the red roan. A red roan is a horse that is red-coloured, sprinkled with little grey hairs. Then there is "Chestnut" who is called that because he is coloured like chestnuts when they are ripe in the fall, and "Teddy," the buckskin horse. He is tan-coloured and has a black stripe on his backbone. Farmer Green got him from the West. There is a little mark called a brand on his flank which tells that.

"Old Methuselah" and "White Boots" do not do much work now. "Old Methuselah" is all white. He was pretty old when Farmer Green bought him so he was nicknamed for the oldest man in the Bible. "White Boots" is a bay mare. That means a red-brown mother horse. She has four white feet. By her side runs a little black colt with funny legs. Jehosophat gave him *his* name, "Black Prince."

"Hal" and "Teddy" and "Chestnut" are very tired for they have been pulling the plough, the wagon, or doing

Robert Gordon Anderson

some farm work all day.

Very glad they are to get their heavy leather collars and harness off and rest in the cool barn. They have hay to eat but they have been working hard so they have oats besides. Jehosophat, Marmaduke, and Hepzebiah eat oats too but theirs are flattened out and cooked. We call it oatmeal. The oats for the horses are not flat but round like little seeds, and are not cooked on any stove. Farmer Green cuts the stalks in the oat field. Then he takes them to the threshing-machine, which knocks the little oats off the stalks. Then they are put in bags to keep for the horses.

But the little black colt with the funny long legs does not eat them. *He* gets milk from his mother. He is just a baby horse, you see, but when he gets bigger he will have oats and hay too.

Now all the animals are busy eating, the pigs with their curly tails, the sheep, the lambs, the cows, the little calves, the horses, and the colt with the funny legs. It is time for the three happy children to have their supper so they run back to the house. Soon, very soon, they will be fast asleep in Slumberland, which is where the Little-Clock-with-the-Wise-Face says you should be now. Good-night.

FIFTH NIGHT

THE TOYMAN

Farmer Green has a man who helps him plough, feed the cows and horses, and with all the work on the farm. His name is Frank, but Jehosophat, Marmaduke, and Hepzebiah call him "the Toyman."

Winter nights around the fire he makes wonderful toys for them.

His knife is like a fairy's wand. With it he whittles boats for Jehosophat, kites for Marmaduke, and dolls for Hepzebiah. He paints them pretty colours too. So I think they gave him the right sort of nickname when they called him "the Toyman."

He hasn't many clothes and no house of his own and no relatives of any sort. He isn't exactly a handsome man. But the three happy children love the Toyman very much.

Yesterday he sat by the edge of the pond. On one side sat Jehosophat, Marmaduke, and big Rover. On the other side sat Hepzebiah, Brownie, and little yellow Wienerwurst.

They were all looking down at the water of the pond. It

Robert Gordon Anderson

was very clear. "Keep still, Wienerwurst," said the Toyman, "or you will scare the fishes."

They were swimming through the waters. Near the banks were little baby fishes, hundreds of them, called minnows. They had a nickname too, "minnies." Out farther, once in a while, the children saw a fish shining like gold. It was a sunfish or "sunny" as they sometimes called it. And the Toyman told them all about these fishes and the perch, too, and the long pickerel and the wicked carp, who hunts the other fish and kills them.

Then all at once the Toyman put his hands in his pockets. Mother Green says his pockets are like ten-cent stores. They are so full of all sorts of things.

The three children watched him closely. First came a piece of wood with a fishline wound around it.

Then with his knife he cut three poles and near the top of each a little notch. The fishlines were tied around the poles. At the other end he put little curved fish-hooks, and about two feet above them little pieces of lead, called "sinkers." The sinkers were to keep the hooks near the bottom of the pond where the fish stay most of the time.

Then from his pockets the Toyman took three pretty things which he had made the night before. They were whittled of wood and shaped like lemons with sharper points. The red and blue one was tied on Jehosophat's line, the red and yellow one on Marmaduke's, and the blue and yellow on little Hepzebiah's.

"What are those pretty things?" asked Marmaduke.

"Floaters," the Toyman answered. "Watch and you will see what we do with them."

"Now you keep still, you Wienerwurst, or we will put you back in the kennel," called the Toyman to the little yellow dog, who felt very frisky and wanted to bark all the time.

By the feet of the Toyman was a tin can. He put in his hand and pulled out a worm. This was put on Jehosophat's hook, another on Marmaduke's, and another on Hepzebiah's.

Then the Toyman threw the three hooks in the water. The two boys held their poles tight but the Toyman had to help little Hepzebiah hold her pole, for her hands were too small.

"Now quiet, everybody!" said the Toyman once more and they all sat watching the red and blue, the yellow and blue, and the red and yellow floaters out on the water.

"When the floater goes under, you will know that a fish is biting at the worm on the hook."

The Toyman had no sooner said this than he called out loud:

"Watch 'er!"

The red and yellow floater was pulled way under the water. The string on Marmaduke's pole tightened and the pole bent.

Three times the floater went under the water.

Robert Gordon Anderson

Then Marmaduke threw his pole back quickly and the hook came out of the water. On it something wriggled. The thing fell plop into Hepzebiah's lap. She screamed while it flopped there. It was a little bigger than the Toyman's hand and round and flat and shiny red and gold. No, it was not a goldfish. It was a sunfish.

After the Toyman had taken the sunfish from the hook and put another worm on it, he threw the line back into the water.

Then all the three children and the two dogs sat watching the little rings in the water around the floaters. Sometimes farther out they saw larger rings, and a fish feeling pretty happy, because of the cool September weather, would jump out of the water and turn a somersault through the air.

Then all of a sudden the blue and yellow floater went under and little Hepzebiah caught a sunfish, too.

Jehosophat felt disappointed because he was the oldest and hadn't caught any fish at all. But the afternoon was not gone when he felt a big tug at his line. It took him a long time to pull that fish in. When the hook came out of the water a long wriggly thing was on it.

"Oo, oo, it's a snake," screamed little Hepzebiah.

"No, it's only an eel," said the Toyman, "he won't hurt you."

But he had to take it off Jehosophat's hook himself, the eel was so slippery and wriggled so. Before the sun went down, the children had each caught two fish.

There were three sunfish, two perch, and the wriggly eel.

The Toyman cleaned them all. And Mother fried them with butter and flour in a pan. It was a good supper they had that night, for they had caught it themselves. When supper was over three little heads were nodding and soon the three happy children were taking a little sail way on into Dreamland. That is a beautiful place where you would like to go too. So you had better follow them quickly. Perhaps you can catch up with them. Good-night.

Robert Gordon Anderson

SIXTH NIGHT

THE WILLOW WHISTLE

The Toyman sat by the pond under the "Crying Tree." That is what Marmaduke calls it, though the Toyman says it is a weeping willow. It's leaves are a very pretty green, much lighter than the leaves of the other trees. And the branches bend over till they reach the water. They really do look like showers of tears. Sometimes little leaves fall into the water and float away like silver-green boats, rowed by tiny fairies.

Jehosophat, Marmaduke, and Hepzebiah came up to the "Crying Tree."

"What are you doing, Toyman," asked Marmaduke.

"Watch and you will see."

They were always asking him that question and he was always telling them to watch and see.

So they did.

In his hand he had his knife, which could make as many things as a fairy's wand. It had four blades and a corkscrew.

The Toyman cut some thin branches from the tree. From these he cut three pieces, each about as long as his first finger and about as thick as his little finger.

One end of each piece of wood he cut like the stern of a boat, then he cut a notch near the end.

Then he worked with his knife very carefully. Soon the green bark came off each little piece of wood. The bark came off whole, like a little roll of green paper.

"See," said the Toyman, "the bark is the skin of the tree and in spring the sap which is the blood of the tree flows fast. It isn't coloured red, it is just like light juice, but it makes the bark slip off this wood very easily."

On the grass he laid the round pieces of green bark. Then he took the white bits of wood which had been under the bark and he whittled away at the ends. Soon he was through.

Then he slipped the pieces of bark, which looked so much like little rolled-up green papers, back on the white pieces of wood.

They fitted perfectly.

One he gave to Jehosophat, one to Marmaduke, and one to Hepzebiah.

"What are they?" asked Marmaduke.

"I know," said his brother Jehosophat, "they are whistles."

"Yes," said the Toyman. "They are willow whistles.

Robert Gordon Anderson

Now put them in your mouths and blow."

Each put the end of his whistle in his mouth and blew.

It sounded very pretty, the three whistles - and then - what do you think?

Not far from the weeping willow or the "Crying Tree," was an elm tree. It was taller than the willow and darker green.

In it something shone very bright - like an orange, only it moved.

"It's an oriole," said the Toyman.

They looked hard and, sure enough, there among the leaves was the prettiest bird they had ever seen. He had an orange-coloured body and black wings.

His nest was on the end of a branch. It was grey-coloured and hung low like a little bag, made of knitted grey wool. Father and Mother Oriole had made it themselves. Mother Oriole is there sitting in it on little eggs.

But Father Oriole heard the three willow whistles and he turned and began to whistle back - oh such a pretty song. It was really prettier than the sound of the three willow whistles for it had different notes and a tune like the songs Mother plays on the piano.

"We must watch that nest," said the Toyman. "Some day soon we will see the baby orioles."

But there - the Little-Clock-with-the-Wise-Face is

scolding again. So the story must stop for tonight.

When you're asleep if you listen very hard, maybe you can hear the three happy children blowing the willow whistles, and maybe the beautiful oriole will answer back.

Good-night.

SEVENTH NIGHT

MR. SCARECROW

Under the big oak by the brook sat the three happy children with Rover, Brownie, and little yellow Wienerwurst. They were watching the Toyman cut the ripe corn.

"Isn't that funny?" said Jehosophat.

"What's funny?" asked Marmaduke.

"Wot's funny?" repeated Hepzebiah.

"Oh! I was just thinking," said Jehosophat, "how he seems just Frank when he's ploughing or harrowing or cutting the corn. But when he's through work and tells us stories or makes us things, why then he is the Toyman."

"Yes," his brother agreed. "He looks as if some fairy godmother changed him nights and Sundays."

But they were rudely interrupted.

"Caw, caw!" said a voice.

It was a rascal's voice.

"Caw, caw!" said another.

The Toyman jumped. He shook his fist.

"You old thief!" he called.

"Rogue, rogue, rogue!" growled Rover in his deep voice.

"Run, run, run!" barked Brownie.

"Rough, rough - rough, rough!" said little Wienerwurst in his funny voice.

"There he is," said the Toyman, "Mr. Jim Crow and all his wicked chums. See there!"

All the children looked in the direction in which his finger pointed. Over in the far corner of the field a flock of crows flew up from the waving corn. A white horse, drawing a buggy, was trotting along the road by the side of the cornfield. The driver had scared Mr. Jim Crow and all his chums. They flapped their big black wings as they flew. And they flew very straight, not like the pretty barn-swallows with their dark-blue wings. The swallow is a happy bird and skims and dances in the air like a fancy skater on the ice. But Mr. Jim Crow flies like an arrow. That is because he is always up to some mischief and forever running away when someone finds him out.

"Caw, caw!" he called.

"Caw, caw!" called all his black mates.

The Toyman ran to the fence and picked up a shotgun.

It had two barrels that shone in the sun.

"Bang, bang!" went the gun.

One black spot dropped to the earth like a stone.

The Toyman ran out in the cornfield. He bent over until his straw hat was hidden by the waving corn.

Soon he came back. From his hand Mr. Jim Crow hung head downward. He was very still.

"Oo, oo! You've hurted him!"

Little Hepzebiah began to cry.

"Don't cry," said the Toyman, patting her head. "Mr. Jim Crow was a bad fellow. You couldn't teach him any lessons."

"What did he do?" Marmaduke asked.

"He stole all the corn and you wouldn't have any nice muffins if he had had his way. I never shoot the orioles or the robins or the swallows or any of the birds with consciences."

"What is a conscience?"

"Oh a little clock inside you, like the Clock-with-the-Wise-Face-on-the-Mantel. It tells you when it is time to stop," explained their friend.

And Jehosophat and Marmaduke looked as if they knew just what he meant. But Hepzebiah was too little yet to understand.

"See, Mr. Jim Crow is long and black. He has a bad eye."

So he buried Mr. Jim Crow under the oak tree while the children watched.

After that the Toyman said:

"I reckon Mr. Scarecrow has fainted."

"Who's Mr. Scarecrow?" asked the three happy children. "Is he Mr. Jim Crow's cousin?"

"Ha, ha, ha!" laughed the Toyman. "That is a good one. No, Mr. Scarecrow is the policeman of the cornfield. Let's go over and set him on his pins again."

So again he walked through the rows between the cornstalks and they came to a little clear place in the middle of the field.

There, flat on his back, lay Mr. Scarecrow.

He too looked as if he were dead. But he was not.

For his body was only two sticks of wood nailed together like a cross. He was dressed in Father Green's old blue trousers and the Toyman's old black coat. His arms were outstretched. But he had lost his hat. His wooden head stuck out.

The Toyman picked him up and stood him straight on his one wooden leg. Then he put the old felt hat on his hard head.

"There, old wooden top," the Toyman spoke to him

Robert Gordon Anderson

sternly. "Don't leave your beat."

But Marmaduke was puzzled.

"How could he scare Mr. Jim Crow away like a policeman? He can't run with that wooden leg."

"Silly," said Jehosophat, for he was older than Marmaduke and knew Mr. Scarecrow very well.

"Ha, ha, ha, that's another good one," said the Toyman. "Of course he can't run. But when all the Crows see him standing up in the cornfield they think he is a real man. They are afraid Mr. Scarecrow will shoot. For they know that things that wear coats and hats often have guns. And guns have killed their chums. So they do not come very near when Mr. Scarecrow is around."

"Caw, caw!" sounded the old rascals again. But the crows were far away. The three happy children could see them way up in the old chestnut tree over on the edge of their neighbour's wood.

In the fork of two high branches was a great round nest - oh ever so much bigger than the thrush's and the oriole's. It was a crow's nest. Sailors often call the little turret built around the mast, where they stand and look out over the sea, a "crow's nest." It looks something like that.

But Mr. Jim Crow's chums didn't come near the cornfield that day.

At night, when they were ready for bed, Jehosophat said to Marmaduke:

"I wonder if old Mr. Scarecrow is out there now."

"Course he is," his brother assured him.

"Let's see!"

So they jumped out of bed and, in their white nightgowns, tiptoed over the floor to the window. The Old-Man-in-the-Moon was up. He looked as round and fat as a pumpkin in the sky.

He winked at them.

The Old-Man-in-the-Moon made it very bright so that they could see.

Sure enough, way out in the cornfield stood Mr. Scarecrow.

His hat and coat were on and he was standing up like a man, very straight and still. His arms were outstretched to tell Mr. Jim Crow's chums that he was ready for them.

But though they are thieves, the Black Crows are not night burglars and they were fast asleep in the nests in the wood.

The Man-in-the-Moon winked at them three times, once with his right eye, once with his left eye, then again with the right.

And the three happy children thought they heard him say three times:

"Back to bed, back to bed, back to bed!"

Robert Gordon Anderson

Then they heard the sound of bells. Seven times they sounded. It was from the church over in the town, - the big white church with the long finger pointing at the sky. And the Little-Clock-with-the-Wise-Face-on-the-Mantel, answered back.

So they obeyed the old yellow Man-in-the-Moon and scampered like little white mice back to bed.

EIGHTH NIGHT

THE PRETTIEST FAIRY STORY IN THE WORLD

"Tell me a story - a fairy story," said Jehosophat to his Mother.

The three happy children loved really true stories and fairy stories too. Sometimes they wanted one, sometimes the other. Sometimes the Toyman mixed his stories up so it was hard to tell which they were.

This morning it was spring. The sun was warm and Jehosophat felt very lazy.

"No," said Mother. "I have too much work to do. But if you will help me dry the dishes I won't tell you but I'll *show you* one of the prettiest fairy stories in the world."

"It is true too," she added.

"Mother, how can that be," said Marmaduke. "A fairy story that is a true story?"

"Just be patient," she replied, "and you will see."

So the boys took the dish towels and helped dry the dishes, without any accidents. But little Hepzebiah was

Robert Gordon Anderson

too small, so she sat on the floor with her finger in her mouth and watched them.

"Come," said Mother Green when they were through.

Out in the vegetable garden, back of the raspberries they went.

"See there," said Mother.

Three square little garden plots with nice brown earth were waiting for seeds.

"Father dug them for you - one for Jehosophat, one for Marmaduke, and one for Hepzebiah."

The three happy children couldn't help but think that was fine.

Just then along came Father.

His arms were full.

He had three little rakes, three little hoes, and three little spades.

The three happy children did not need to ask whom they were for.

"But where's the fairy story, Mother?"

"That you will make," she said. "The jolly old Sun, the gentle Rain, and brown Mother Earth will help you."

Jehosophat laughed.

"Oh! I see now. But we can't finish that fairy story all in one day."

"No, it takes time and it takes work. But it's a prettier story than any in books. And you can make it come true yourselves."

Then Marmaduke piped up:

"What do we do first?"

"Well," his Mother explained, "your Father has dug the ground for you. You must rake it first, make it smooth and even. Mind, no hard lumps now!"

So the three happy children set to work with their three shiny rakes. Father had to help Hepzebiah, of course.

Then when the earth was smooth and fine, like brown powder, they made little furrows or lines in the earth. In other parts of the little gardens they scooped out tiny holes with their hoes.

Out of his pockets Father took some square envelopes. On them were printed pretty flowers and ripe vegetables.

"There," said Mother, "are the pictures of the *end* of the fairy story. But you'll never know the end unless you try hard."

Father tore open the envelopes and sowed the seeds in Hepzebiah's garden, some in the little holes, some in the furrows. Then he let the two boys sow their own gardens.

Robert Gordon Anderson

After the envelopes were all empty and the seeds all scattered they covered them over with the fine brown soil.

"The little seeds must sleep for a while," said their Mother, "like babies in a big brown bed."

So every day the three children watched. And the Sun shone and sometimes the gentle Rain came. They did not feel sad when she was weeping, for Mother told them she was a fairy too, not so jolly as the Sun but gentle and kind. Jolly Sun, gentle Rain, and Mother Earth - they were all fairies whom God had sent to help make the story come true.

Sometimes it was hard to finish breakfast, they were so anxious to see what had happened in the little gardens during the night. Sometimes they even forgot to ask Mother to "please excuse" them and they had to be called back to the table, for that was very impolite.

At last one wonderful morning, as they stood around the flower beds, Jehosophat said:

"There's Chapter Two!"

"What's that?" asked Marmaduke who didn't quite understand.

"Oh, just another step in the fairy tale."

"Where?"

He pointed to one of the gardens.

From the brown earth a little green head poked out.

Little Hepzebiah danced for it was in her garden, and toddled off to tell Mother.

Next day there were five more little heads, some in each of the gardens. They were light in colour and seemed weak but somehow the jolly old Sun and brown Mother Earth took care of them as parents take care of babies. And sometimes the gentle Rain came to water them with her tears. So they grew strong and soon the gardens were covered with an army of sturdy little green spears.

"It looks like a brown pincushion with green needles and pins," said Jehosophat.

And the weeks passed and still the three good fairies worked hard over them to help them live and grow up to be real vegetables and flowers. They worked away very quietly, these three good fairies, as all good people work, without any noise, without any fuss.

One day Farmer Green came back from a visit to the town.

With him he brought three green watering-pots.

"You must do some more work, yourselves," he told them as he handed each one of the shiny green cans. "You must water them when the Rain fairy is tired, pull up the bad weeds that steal the food Mother Earth keeps for the flowers, and you must keep the soil loose around the roots, so that the drops can sink way down deep. The more work you do the better you will like your flowers when they do come. And the taller and prettier they will be."

Robert Gordon Anderson

So the little green stalks grew tall and strong. Then the little buds came.

And one by one the buds opened into flowers. And the flowers had on their petals all the colours of the rainbow in the sky.

And the children took turns filling the vase on the supper table. They were very proud of their flowers when their father leaned over and smelled them.

"My, how sweet they smell!" he would say every time. "I don't think I *ever* saw such flowers."

And when their vegetables came to the table - round plump red radishes, crisp curling lettuce leaves, juicy tomatoes, and rows of peas in the pod, like the little toes of the neighbour's baby, Father Green would say:

"I never did eat such vegetables!"

Then he would smile over at Mother.

And Marmaduke, after his turn one night, whispered to his mother -

"It *was* a pretty fairy story, Mother. And we made it come true ourselves."

"Yes, with the help of God and His fairies - the jolly Sun, the gentle Rain, and brown Mother Earth. But the best part of it all is that *your own* hands helped."

But the Little-Clock-with-the-Wise-Face-on-the-Mantle thought that the children understood now. So he stopped this advice with his silver tongue.

And Mother, too, agreed that it was late. So she kissed them good-night and tucked them under the coverlids as they had covered the tiny seeds in their brown beds.

NINTH NIGHT

ANOTHER TRUE FAIRY STORY

Jehosophat, Marmaduke, and Hepzebiah were very happy as they watched the fairy story of the flowers. They were happier still because they helped it grow. But of course that did not take all of their time. So one morning when Marmaduke had eaten up all of his oatmeal and the cream, which Buttercup had given him, he laid his spoon down and said:

"Won't you show us another story, 'cause we can't watch our gardens all day long?"

"Yes," said Mother, "let me think what it will be."

So Mother thought awhile.

"I'll get Mother Nature to show you another story. But you can't help with this one. You'll just have to watch. It's made by the birds themselves."

Then she looked at the calendar.

"Why, it's the fourteenth of May. He ought to be here pretty soon."

"Who ought to be here soon?" asked Jehosophat.

"Why, the Oriole, the Baltimore Oriole, on his way back from the South, where he lives all winter."

"How do you know he'll come soon?" the three children asked, all in the same breath.

"He always comes back about the middle of May. City folks call May first 'Moving Day,' but the fifteenth is the Oriole's Moving Day."

So Mother led them out of the front door.

"Just sit in that swing or play with the pine needles and watch that elm. Don't make too much noise now! Maybe he'll come today."

And the children played in the front of the house all the morning and looked up at the dark green leaves of the elm every once in a while. But no bright little bird messenger came.

They were very much disappointed but Mother said:

"Never mind, tomorrow is his Moving Day and I think he'll come then. He is usually pretty prompt."

That night Uncle Roger came to the house with Aunt Mehitable. As a special treat the children were allowed to stay up late and hear Uncle Roger's stories of the great sea.

They stayed up very late, although the Little-Clock-with-the-Wise-Face-on-the-Mantle spoke several times. So next morning they were very tired. The sun was warm and while Jehosophat, Marmaduke and Hepzebiah sat on the porch they fell asleep.

Jehosophat's head nodded against one post, Marmaduke's against another post, while little Hepzebiah fell asleep between them on the floor of the porch.

"Wow, wow, wow," growled Rover, "let's go out in the barnyard and chase the White Wyandottes. It's no fun playing with sleepy children."

"Wow, wow, wow!" answered Brownie and little Wienerwurst together, and this in dog's language means "Yes."

So they romped away to the barnyard to chase the frightened White Wyandottes.

That was not a good thing for the chickens but it was a good thing for the children. For if the dogs had not run away they might have missed something very wonderful.

What do you think it was?

First they heard pretty strains of music. It was something like a song and something like a whistle.

They looked up in the elm tree.

There, shining among the dark green leaves, was a pretty thing with orange and black feathers. He whistled away as if he did not have a care in the world.

And they did not have to be told - they knew who it was. It was their old friend, the Oriole.

He didn't stay still very long ever, for he was a busy fellow. But once he swung on a twig for a little while.

They saw that he was almost as big as a robin, with head and shoulders of black, the wings black too, and most of his tail. But the rest of his body was like the prettiest orange-coloured velvet they had ever seen. He was singing something like this:

"What a fine day, what a fine day.
I can sing and build, for work is play."

And every once in a while he would fly over to the apple tree and hop from branch to branch between the pink and white blossoms, looking for food. He was very fond of those caterpillars in the tree, you see. In between mouthfuls he would whistle just part of his song,

"A-ver-y-fine-day!"

Then he would take another bite, hop to another branch and whistle again:

"A-ver-y-fine-day!"

He certainly seemed to be happy over the beautiful weather.

Then he would whistle again as if he were talking to someone.

The three sleepy children listened.

"Now that nest, dear, now that nest, dear. We must build that nest, before we rest."

To whom could he be talking?

Robert Gordon Anderson

They looked around. And there, hopping about on a spray of beautiful apple blossoms, was another bird. It was Mother Oriole. She was almost like Father Oriole, only her coat was not as bright as his. It is funny the way birds are dressed, isn't it? What would you think if some Sunday *your* Father went to church in a black coat with a yellow vest, while Mother wore some very dull colour? You would laugh. But that is the way with birds. The father bird always wears brighter colours than the mother.

The three happy children were glad that the mother bird had come with the father bird up from the sunny South. They heard him whistle again:

"In the Winter we go South, dear,
But in the Spring to the North we wing."

Then together they flew back to the elm. They were house-hunting. Back on the roof of the barn there was a little house of wood with doors for the pretty pigeons, but there were no houses of any kind on the old elm. Still the Orioles did not worry about that. They were not lazy, oh no!

They were just looking for a place to build. They must have found it, for the Oriole sang again (he was always changing his song):

"My dear, my dear,
Sunny - quiet - lovely - here."

He had chosen a branch about thirty feet from the ground. Mother Oriole quietly answered back that it suited her perfectly. They both flew down to the ground, then back to the tree. And every time they travelled they had little pieces of grass or bark in their bills. But Mother Oriole did most of this work, which was quite proper, for mothers always do most of the work about the house, don't they? Father Oriole, you see, was more interested in getting fat beetles and caterpillars for food. And that was quite right too. But once he sang out louder than ever, for he had found a bit of string from Jehosophat's broken kite.

"The very thing, the very thing," he said to her.

And once Mother Oriole found, caught in the shutter, little threads of Hepzebiah's hair.

Then the three happy children woke up. They rubbed their eyes. They had been dreaming in the warm sun.

But their dream was true and the fairy story was true.

For there were the two birds, very pretty and very much alive. They were busily flying to the earth again and back to the elm branch. And they were carrying the materials for their new home in their beaks.

They perched on the branch and crocheted with their beaks. Yes, crocheted the little bits of bark and string and grass and hair into a tiny nest. Hanging down from the branch, it looked like the pretty soft grey bags which ladies carry, only it was very small.

And between whiles Father Oriole would whistle in delight and Mother Oriole would answer back quietly.

They were very happy birds and were quite content with the warm sun and the cool elm leaves and the pretty apple blossoms and their breakfast and dinner

Robert Gordon Anderson

and supper. And they were very grateful to the good God who had given these things to them, grateful and happy as all little children should be.

But that is not the end of the fairy story. No, that is - but the Little-Clock-with-the-Wise-Face-on-the-Mantel won't let us tell any more. His silver voice says:

"Ting - ting - ting - ting - ting - ting - ting," which means:

"Tell - that - tale - a - noth - er - time."

So good-night.

TENTH NIGHT

THE HAPPY ENDING OF THE ORIOLE'S STORY

All stories should have an ending. It's fine, isn't it, when they end happily?

And this story of the Orioles did end happily - oh, so happily!

It was this way, you see.

The little grey house on the elm was finished.

It hung down from the end of the green branch, under the leaves. It looked both like a fairy house and a little crocheted bag.

Now for some days Mother Oriole didn't go out very much. She stayed in her little house.

But Father Oriole kept about his work, hunting for the little brown crawling things and the green crawling things that made their food.

He would whistle every once in a while to tell Mother Oriole that he was near. Sometimes it was just a few notes to say:

Robert Gordon Anderson

"I'm still here - my dear,
Still here, still here, still here."

Sometimes:

"All right, my love!"

Sometimes just:

"All's well!"

But if a strange man came too near the tree his song was sharp and angry.

"Look out, look out, look out!
He's a rogue, an awful rogue, look out, I say!"

But somehow he didn't seem to mind the children.

"Why does Mother Oriole sit so quietly on her nest?" Marmaduke asked his own mother.

"I wish I could lift you up so that you could see. But the nest is too high up. It's out of harm's way. Dicky Means, who has a cruel heart and robs birds' nests, can't reach it way up there!"

"What's in it, Muvver?" asked little Hepzebiah. You see her little tongue didn't work just right. She never could say words with "th" in them.

"Little eggs, dear. They are white, with little dark spots and funny dark scrawls on them as if somebody had tried to write with a bad pen."

Then Marmaduke asked:

"And is she keeping them warm?"

"Yes, so that they will hatch out. They will, very soon now."

So for a number of days in the warm weather, and in the rainy weather too, Mother Oriole sat faithfully on her nest. Bird mothers and the mothers of little children are always very patient. Then came one fine morning when the sun was particularly jolly and bright, and the blossoms smelt very sweet and were beginning to fall from the trees. The three happy children stood under the elm and looked up at the tiny hanging nest.

They heard new noises, strange noises.

It sounded like babies.

Yes, the little Oriole babies had broken their shells and had been born at last.

They didn't have many clothes on. But some day their feathers will be as pretty as their father's.

How they did cry for food! Somehow baby Orioles cry more than other bird babies. They seem to want to eat all the time.

And how Father Oriole did work to keep them fed, whistling every once in a while to make things pleasant for his family! I wonder if they appreciated all the things he and Mother Oriole did for them. And the days passed and the little birds grew fatter on the bugs and the beetles which their father brought, just as fat as the little boys or girls on their oatmeal and bread and milk, which their fathers work hard to earn for them.

The little Orioles were certainly noisy little birds, and when they cried sometimes the children saw funny little heads and beaks poking out of the nest.

Then more days passed and Father and Mother Oriole taught them to fly, just as Father and Mother Green had taught little Hepzebiah to walk. Marmaduke remembered how his Mother had held Hepzebiah and Father stood a little way off. Then Hepzebiah had started. She was a little frightened at first but she made the journey. It was only a few steps and her father caught her before she fell. She tried this often and soon she could take a great many steps.

And that was something like the way Father and Mother Oriole taught their children to fly. The parent birds would fly to a branch a little way off. Then they would call the little birds. And one by one they would fly to the branch. Their wings were weak at first like Hepzebiah's little feet. But soon they grew strong and before many weeks had gone they could fly as fast as the old birds. And before the summer was over they were as big as their parents. You see birds have shorter lives than real people. They do not live so many years. So they have to grow up quickly or they wouldn't have much time for work and play, would they?

So the children decided that the story of the Orioles was a very pretty fairy story, indeed, and they liked it better because it was true.

And they found others - oh, so many stories like it.

For sometimes Mother and sometimes Father and

sometimes the Toyman showed them other little bird homes.

They climbed a ladder and found the barn-swallow's nest plastered under the eaves of the barn. They liked the barn swallow who flew through the air, almost as if he were so happy that he danced as he flew. And his dress was so pretty, for he was dark blue on top, brown on the throat, and his little stomach was white. His tail was forked too, cut like the coat of the man in the circus who cracked the whip and made the horses perform tricks.

The barn swallow's nest was so cunningly made. It was plastered of mud and grass, and had a soft grass lining. The little eggs in it were white and had tiny brown spots.

Right near the bay window, in the thick lilac tree, Marmaduke spied Red Robin's nest. He was a great friend of theirs. They always liked the cheery way he hopped over the lawn, and his cheery red vest, and his song which always said:

"Che-eer up - che-eer up!"

His eggs were the prettiest of all, a greenish blue, a robin's-egg blue, the dressmakers call it. Mother Green's summer dress was coloured just like it.

And in a bush by the roadside, Hepzebiah spied the brown thrush's nest. His eggs were blue and spotted with brown.

And in the elderberry tree they found the grey cat-bird's nest. He was a funny bird, always crying like a

Robert Gordon Anderson

lost pussy. And his eggs were green-blue.

So in the fields and the woods Jehosophat, Marmaduke and Hepzebiah saw all kinds of birds and all kinds of nests and all kinds of eggs. They saw them because their eyes were bright and sharp as yours must be too when you go into the beautiful country.

And from the eggs funny little birds were born and grew up and flew and sang.

And so the three happy children decided that the really true fairy stories of Mother Nature were the prettiest of all.

And oh - we almost forgot! Perhaps we can tell the rest before that Little-Clock-with-the-Wise-Face-on-the-Mantel tells us to stop.

Over near Neighbour Brown's fence they were peeping through the green leaves at the song-sparrow's nest. Mother was with them and they saw someone come out of their neighbour's house.

"Wouldn't you like to see her?" the strange lady whispered to Mother.

"Oh yes," Mother whispered back, "but they mustn't wake her up."

Who could they be talking about? Then they went through the gate.

"Be very quiet," said Mother as they entered the door, "and you'll see the end of another true fairy story."

So they tiptoed in.

There in a bed lay Mrs. Brown, looking very happy.

And curled up in her arm she had - well, what do you think she had?

A little sleeping baby!

Like the little Orioles Baby had been born just a few days ago.

"That," said Mother, "is the prettiest fairy story of all."

And the children thought so too.

There - we've finished just in time. We hear the Little Clock. There goes his silver tongue now.

Good-night! Sweet Dreams.

ELEVENTH NIGHT

MOTHER HEN AND ROBBER HAWK

Jehosophat and Marmaduke were whispering together.

"Let's try it," said Jehosophat.

"An' see what happens," added Marmaduke.

So they tiptoed into the House of the White Wyandottes and placed the big duck's eggs in with the smaller eggs under the setting hen.

Mother Hen did not like that, oh no!

She stirred in her nest. All her feathers puffed up and she looked very much hurt.

"Duck, duck, duck!" sniffed she scornfully. And to herself she added: "What a mean way to treat a decent, respectable hen!" For White Wyandottes are very particular and very exclusive.

But after the two little imps had tiptoed out of her house, she made the best of a bad matter. She couldn't kick the big duck's eggs out of the nest in the box. The sides of the box were too high. So she settled down on her eggs again.

"I must keep my very own warm, anyway," she decided.

About three weeks later there was much excitement in the House of the White Wyandottes. From the nest in the box came little noises.

"Chip, chip, chip," sounded faintly from inside the eggs. And before the sun climbed over the Big Gold Rooster, who swung on the weather-vane on the barn, all the new little chickens had broken their eggs.

"How nice it is to be born!" they cheeped together in a merry chorus, as they arrived in the wonderful world.

Very proud of her family was Mother Wyandotte when the little yellow balls began to run about. A few days later she was prouder still when they scampered this way and that, pecking at little bugs and ants. They worked hard for their breakfasts and dinners and suppers.

Even Father Wyandotte, the great white rooster with the magnificent red comb and curling white plumes on his tail, forgot that other rooster of whom he was so jealous. For the rooster who was always perched on the weather-vane on the barn was up so high and he shone like gold.

But now Father Wyandotte was not jealous. He walked around in his lordly way, cocking his eye at his little yellow sons and daughters as they chased the fat little bugs.

At first he would not say just how proud of them he was. He did not like to tell all his feelings at once.

Robert Gordon Anderson

Sometimes he thought fighting and crowing better than being a family man. But all of a sudden he flew up on the tallest fence-post he could find, and flapped his wings. He threw back his head, opened his yellow beak, and crowed up at that gold rooster:

"Sure, sure, sure! You couldn't do it, you couldn't do it - couldn't do it, do."

No, the Gold Rooster on the weather-vane on the top of the barn, though he shone like the sun, could neither crow nor raise a family.

But Mother Wyandotte didn't bother about anything so high in the sky as the sun and the rooster. She was busy playing nurse-maid to her little yellow children and helping them find food.

But in the afternoon she did look up at the sky. That was when something like a dark shadow sailed in the air far above the home of the White Wyandottes.

It was a great bird with wide-stretched wings, much bigger than Jim Crow. He sailed in circles, while his evil eye looked down at the frightened, scampering White Wyandottes.

"Um!" How he would like a nice chicken for lunch!

"Robber Hawk!" called all of Mother Hen's uncles and aunts in the barnyard.

"Robber Hawk!" screamed all of her great-uncles and great-aunts too.

"Robber Hawk!" screamed all of her cousins, first,

second, and third.

Loud and long barked Rover and Brownie. And little Wienerwurst stopped chasing the pretty pink pigeons.

And even Mr. Stuckup, the turkey, had to join in the hubbub.

"Horrible robber, horrible robber," he gobbled.

But Mother Wyandotte had called to her children. She opened her wings and under them quickly in fright they ran, all huddling together. Her wings hardly seemed large enough to cover them all, but she took them all in, every one of her children.

She was a nervous old thing, but she was a good mother, and good mother hens, good animal mothers, and our own mothers too, never seem to think of themselves when there is danger around. They just look out for their little ones.

"Robber Hawk, robber! Shan't touch 'em - robber!" she said.

Then - quick as a wink - there was another loud noise, just like that day when Jim Crow fell in the cornfield.

"Bang, bang!"

Jehosophat, Marmaduke and Hepzebiah jumped.

They looked around.

There stood the Toyman with the gun at his shoulder.

Robert Gordon Anderson

Little puffs of smoke like white feathers floated away from the muzzles of the gun.

"Winged him, anyway!" cried the Toyman.

They looked up.

Robber Hawk wasn't sailing in the sky any longer.

He was falling, falling, like a stone - just like Jim Crow.

"The Toyman's a good shot," exclaimed Jehosophat. "My, how I wish I could shoot like that!"

Mother Green came to the back door.

She called to the Toyman:

"He's fallen on the barn, Frank."

"Roof, roof, roof!" barked little Wienerwurst to explain it more clearly.

Sure enough, Robber Hawk dropped on the roof of the barn, right by the Gold Rooster who swung on the weather-vane.

The Toyman scratched his head.

"Quite a climb for these stiff legs," said he.

But he fetched a tall ladder and placed it against the side of the barn.

The three children watched him, their heads bent back

so far that they almost snapped off.

Mother held the ladder at the foot, for nobody wanted anything ever to happen to the Toyman.

"Careful!" she warned him.

"All right, Mis' Green," he said. "I haven't been up in the maintop for nothing."

You see, once upon a time, he had been a sailor. There was nothing that the Toyman hadn't done.

He reached the top of the ladder, then swung out on the roof. At last he reached the ridge.

There stood the Gold Rooster, never crowing or saying anything at all. And under him lay Robber Hawk, and he didn't say anything either.

Carefully the Toyman climbed down from the ridge of the barn, holding the rascal in his hands. Then one by one down the rungs of the ladder he came.

When he reached the ground Jehosophat, Marmaduke and Hepzebiah gathered round.

Robber Hawk hung limp from the Toyman's hand.

His dark brown feathers never stirred. His white breast with its dark bars and patches never moved.

"Robber Hawk," spoke the Toyman, "your old curved beak will never feed on any more good chicken."

Then he turned to the children.

Robert Gordon Anderson

"We must bury him by Jim Crow."

So Jehosophat, Marmaduke, Hepzebiah, Rover, Brownie, Wienerwurst and the Toyman marched with Robber Hawk on towards the cornfield.

There by the side of Jim Crow they buried him.

And the Toyman took two pieces of wood. On these he cut with his knife:

JIM CROW
KILLED 1918
THIEF

ROBBER HAWK
KILLED 1918
THIEF AND MURDERER

At their heads he placed the two boards side by side.

"There we will leave them," the Toyman spoke sternly, "as a warning to all evil-doers."

So they walked back slowly to the House of the White Wyandottes where Mother Hen clucked contentedly once more and all the yellow chickens ran around, chasing the little bugs in their game of hide-and-seek. A fine game it was too, only it was more interesting for the chickens than the bugs, you see.

The three happy children noticed that one of the little yellow fellows was larger than the others. He -

"Ting - ting - ting - ting - ting - ting - ting!"

"End - that - tale - to - mor - row - night."

So says the Little Clock. He must be obeyed. So good-bye for a little while.

Robert Gordon Anderson

TWELFTH NIGHT

ABOUT DUCKIE THE STEPCHILD
AND THE LITTLE SHIP

In the door of the workshop stood the three happy children, watching the Toyman.

It was one of the very nicest places on the whole farm. Tools of all sorts, bright and sharp, lay on the table. Lumber of every kind lay piled against the walls. The shelves were filled with cans of paint. All the colours of the rainbow were in those cans. The children could tell that by the pretty splashes of the paint dripping down their sides.

Back and forth, back and forth swung the arms of the Toyman. He was very busy over something - something very important it must be, for he never talked, only worked and whistled away.

"Oh dear! I wish I knew what it was," sighed Marmaduke. Anyway he knew it was something for *them*. Father Green had given the Toyman a holiday, all for himself, to do as he liked. And *of course* he'd make something for *them*.

On the edge of the table was a vise, a big tool with iron jaws. In the iron jaws was a block of wood. The

Toyman screwed the vise - very tight - so tight the wood couldn't budge. Then he shaved this side of the block, then the other side, with a plane, a tool with a very sharp edge. Clean white shavings fell on the floor, some of them twisting like Hepzebiah's curls.

"I wonder what it's going to be," Marmaduke repeated.

Jehosophat was pretty sure he knew.

"I'll bet it's a boat," he said.

The Toyman chuckled.

"Right you are, Son. It's the Good Ship - well, let's see. All boats have a name, you know. What do you think would be a good name for a fine ship?"

Jehosophat had one, right on the tip of his tongue.

"The Arrow."

The Toyman thought this over.

"That isn't bad," said he.

Then he turned to Marmaduke.

"What's your idea for a name, little chap?"

Marmaduke thought and thought. He looked out through the door and saw the Party Bird, the vain Peacock, parading up and down, showing off its beautiful tail, and "Peacock" was the only name he could think of.

Jehosophat laughed out loud.

"That's no name for a boat."

And Marmaduke had to shout back - as little boys will, losing his temper:

"*'Tis too!*"

The Toyman stopped the quarrel, just as he always did, with something pleasant or funny he said. Then he leaned over and picked up three chips of wood.

"I'll write the names on these little chips," he explained, "and we'll choose."

Putting his hand on Hepzebiah's sunny curls, he asked that little girl:

"What name do *you* think would be nice for the boat?"

Now Hepzebiah really didn't know just what it all was about. But she had heard Marmaduke say "Peacock," so she took her finger out of her mouth just long enough to point at the Guinea-hen, who was screeching horribly out in the barnyard.

"The Guinea-hen! Ha, ha! That's a good one!" The Toyman was forever saying that and laughing at the funny things the children said.

Hepzebiah, thinking that this was a nice sort of a game, took her finger out of her mouth and pointed again - this time out at the pond where the swans were sailing, like pretty white ships themselves.

"The very thing," exclaimed the Toyman. "White Swan's a *fine* name for a boat!"

And he wrote "White Swan" on one chip, "Peacock" on another, and "Arrow" on the last. Then he held them towards the children.

"The smallest must choose first," he said, and Hepzebiah took one of the little white pieces of wood from the Toyman's hand. He turned it over and read:

"White Swan."

"We'd go a good ways before we'd get a better name," he decided. "When the boat's all finished and all sails set, she'll sail away just like a swan; you see if she doesn't."

The hull of the boat was finished now, and on the bow, at the very front, he nailed a thin little stick, with tiny nails. This was the bowsprit.

On the keel at the very bottom, he fastened a piece of lead so she wouldn't "turn turtle" - turn over, he meant, when her sails were set and the wind blew too hard.

Then choosing some sticks - very carefully, for they must be straight - he tucked the boat under his arm and, with the three children close at his heels, walked over to the pond and sat down under the Crying Tree, where the sun shone bright and warm.

Out came the magic knife and he whittled away at the little sticks; whittled and whistled and smiled all the time.

Robert Gordon Anderson

Sliver after sliver of the wood fell on the ground. Sometimes one would drop into the water and float away like a fairy canoe, with the green willow leaves that fell from the Crying Tree.

So under the magic knife the little ship grew and grew, till the masts were fitted too, and set fast and tight in the clean smooth deck.

"But where are the sails?" asked Jehosophat impatiently.

A funny answer the Toyman made.

He just said:

"Hold your horses, Sonny."

The teacher in the Red Schoolhouse up the road would have reproved him for this, but the children thought whatever the Toyman said was all right.

Of course he meant not to be too impatient and - but just then the dinner horn sounded, way out over the pond and over the fields, and the children ran into the house, just as you would have done too.

It didn't take long to finish dinner that day. For desert they had blackberry pie, very juicy and nice, and they didn't even wait to wash the red marks of that pie from their faces but just ran for the Crying Tree.

The Toyman felt in all of his six big pockets. And out came needles and thread, and pieces of clean muslin besides.

Stitch, stitch, stitch went his fingers, for a thousand stitches or more. And bye and bye the sails were all cut and sewed and fitted on the three little masts.

Then the Toyman stopped.

"We haven't christened her yet," he said. "We should have done that long ago."

In his pockets he rummaged again, those pockets which always held just the right thing. It was a small bottle this time, all filled with tiny pink pills. Much nicer these were, the children thought, than that yellow stuff in the big bottle they hated so.

The Toyman poured the little pills out.

"What's the use of medicine on a nice day like this," said he.

And he filled the bottle with water and put back the stopper.

"When ships are launched," he explained, "folks break a bottle over the bow when they name her."

"All right, I'll do that," said Jehosophat, but the Toyman stopped him.

"Hold on there, Sonny, that's the *ladies'* job."

Then he called Hepzebiah and gave her the bottle.

"Now, little girl, you stand here and say: 'I christen thee White Swan.'"

But, "I ckwithen Wite Thwan" was the best she could do.

"Now drop the bottle!"

She opened her fingers and, sure enough, the little bottle fell right on the deck and broke all in little pieces, and the glistening drops splashed over the bow, and so the good ship "White Swan" got her name.

Into the water the Toyman pushed the little ship. The wind filled her sails and off she went, racing away before the wind to join the beautiful birds for whom she had been named.

Around the pond and over the bridge went the Toyman, to the other side. When the ship reached the opposite shore he swung it around and sent it back on the return voyage. The "White Swan" had reached port safely, when the Toyman said:

"It's funny what different opinions folks have. Some like the water and some don't. Now the swans and the ducks, and that little ship, and the fish, and the froggies, and Uncle Roger, and you and I, we think it's fine. But Mr. Stuck-up, and Miss Crosspatch, and Old Mother Wyandotte, and Mis' Fizzeltree, why they won't go near it at all."

"That *is* funny," said Jehosophat.

Then the Toyman added:

"Just listen to that."

Old Mother Wyandotte was right near them, clucking

in fright.

"Don't - don't - don't you do it!" she was calling to one of her children who was looking longingly at the cool pond.

Around her were all her children, fast growing up now. They were all soft and white but one. Like good little chickens they were looking for bugs, all but one.

He was the little fellow they had noticed before, the funny little fellow with a longer bill than the rest, and the odd-looking feet. His soft downy back was turning black. And he was starting for that pretty water shining in the pond.

Jehosophat looked him all over.

"Why, he looks like a duck."

"What did you expect?" laughed the Toyman. "He is a duck. Old Mother Wyandotte thinks he's her child, but he's only a step-child. Ha! Ha! Somebody must have put another egg in her nest."

Over in the garden were pretty flowers called Bleeding Hearts. They were very pink, and Jehosophat's face turned the very same colour. Well *he* knew who had stolen into the House of the White Wyandottes and put that big duck's egg under Old Mother Hen. And now it had turned out a real little duckling, that black little fellow Mother Wyandotte was scolding so.

"Don't - don't - don't - don't you do it," she was shouting still.

Robert Gordon Anderson

But little black Duckie had made up his mind. He was headed straight for that shining water.   ·

Around Mother Wyandotte gathered all her relatives to talk over the matter. They were disgusted. That one of their family should disgrace them so!

"Respectable chickens spend their time on the ground," said Granny Wyandotte with a toss of her comb, "and never, never get wet, if they can help it, not even their feet."

"True - true - quite true," all the Wyandotte Aunties agreed.

But their second cousins and the third cousins too, the ducks and the geese and the swans, said they were wrong.

"Little Duckie's a sensible chap. What better place can there be to play in than that nice cool pond?"

And all the fishes swimming around, from the big pickerel down to the littlest "minnie," waggled their fins and tails to show they agreed too, while the froggies on the lily-pad croaked:

"Gomme on - gomme on!"

They were giving little Duckie a warm invitation to play in the water, you see.

Duckie was right at the edge now and Mother Hen, who was really his step-mother, made one last appeal, but the ducks one and all called:

"Back, back, back!"

They weren't talking to Duckie. They meant the White Wyandottes. They were taking his part, you see, though not for one minute did they guess he was *their* child, *their very own.*

Duckie appreciated that too. Perhaps Old Father Drake, the head of all the Duck family, wouldn't let Step-father Wyandotte punish him that night if he did try the water.

I don't believe Step-father Wyandotte really cared very much. At first he was a little mad but, after scolding a little, he shouted:

"Through, through, through - I'm through with yoooooooouuu."

He wouldn't have anything more to do with little Duckie. I guess he suspected he was just a step-child after all. So he just grumbled to himself as he speared a fat tumble-bug with his beak:

"Ur, ur - I don't care!"

He had enough children anyway. But the Gold Rooster on the top of the barn looked down, laughing at him. He couldn't really laugh, you know, or flap his wings, but he swung from west to southwest and back again, as if to say:

"I knew it. I knew it. They fooled you!"

Old Father Drake, the head of the duck family, started for the water. Mother Duck and all the little ducks went in too. They were going to show Duckie the way.

He just couldn't stand it any longer. So - *plopp* in he went and paddled around after the others, and ducked his head under the water to catch his dinner, just as a real duckling should.

"Better than grubbing for bugs in the dirty earth, this nice clean cool water," quacked he, and he was as happy as happy could be.

The Toyman was looking at him with a smile on his face.

"He's just like me," he said at last, and the children, surprised at that, asked all together:

"*Who's* like you?"

"That little duck there."

"Like you!" Jehosophat shouted. "Why he doesn't look like you at all!"

The Toyman puffed away on his corncob pipe before he answered:

"Oh *inside* he's the same. I was just like him when I was a kid. I had a step-mother, too, and she and all the step-uncles and aunts scolded and scolded, and whipped me besides, because *I* wanted to go to sea on a great big ship."

"What did you do?"

They didn't really need to ask that question, for hadn't

the Toyman been most everywhere, and hadn't he told them many a story about the great sea and the ships?

"Yes, they all said I would drown or become a wicked bad man."

Marmaduke thought he would like to do something to those step-uncles and aunts who treated the Toyman so badly.

"They don't know what they're talking about," he shouted. "You're good as anybody in the world."

"Thank you, little feller," replied the Toyman, patting his head. "But they said I would, just the same. They talked just like those old Wyandottes there.

"But I fooled them all," he went on. "And one night, when it was dark, just a few stars out, I climbed out of bed and jumped out of the window and ran away.

"I walked and I walked, miles and miles, till I came to a big town by the sea. There were lots of big ships at the docks, and I asked a man, with a great big beard, to take me too. So he took me on board, and I was a little cabin boy. But bye and bye I got to be a real sailor, and I sailed all over the world in the ship, and saw lots of people, yellow, and black, and brown, and funny places and queer houses and -"

"Be careful, Frank!"

They all turned at once. There was Mother, standing right near them. All the time she had been listening, near the Crying Tree.

Robert Gordon Anderson

"Now, Frank," she repeated, "be careful or you'll put *notions* in those children's heads, and some day they'll be running away from *me*."

Still she didn't look cross, and she smiled at the Toyman, especially when he answered:

"Not from a mother like you, Mis' Green. How about it, kiddies?"

And Marmaduke and Jehosophat were very sure they never could run away - not even to sea in a beautiful ship. So they kissed her and hugged her too.

Now the froggies were singing their evening song. The sun was getting close to his home in the west. Little Duckie and his real mother and father came out of the water and waddled off towards the barn. The Swans folded their wings and came to the shore. So the Toyman brought the ship to the harbour and anchored her for the night.

THIRTEENTH NIGHT

THE TALL ENEMY

It was the first snowfall. The grey sky was filled with little white feathers dancing down - down - down.

"Look at the snowflakes," exclaimed the three happy children, all in one breath.

"Yes," said their Mother, "the snow has come. In the spring and summer Mother Earth works very hard. It takes so much of her strength, feeding the millions of plants from her brown breast. By fall she is very tired and in winter she takes things quite easy.

"Then the gentle Rain Fairy feels sorry for Mother Earth. She turns her own tears to snow-flakes, and scatters them over her. They weave a soft white comforter to keep her warm. And it keeps the seed babies, sleeping in Mother Earth's brown breast, all snug and warm too."

All that day and all night the snow fell. And all the next day and the next night - and the third day and the third night too.

Then all of a sudden it stopped, and the three happy children woke in the morning, and looked out of

Robert Gordon Anderson

the window.

"Why the snow's most as high as Wienerwurst's house!" cried Jehosophat.

Then they all trooped in to breakfast.

"We will make forts," said Jehosophat.

"Hooray!" exclaimed Marmaduke.

"The very thing!" added Mother.

And Wienerwurst, curled up by the rosy kitchen stove, barked, "Woof, woof, woof."

Now this means a lot of things. But this time it meant, "Good, good, good."

So the three happy children hurried through their oatmeal. They hurried so fast that they had three little pains. Jehosophat had one right under his belt, Marmaduke one in the centre of his blouse, Hepzebiah one under her little red waist.

Mother came in from the kitchen. She looked at the empty bowls.

"What! All gone already! Look out or you'll each have to take a big table-spoonful of the yellow stuff in that bottle."

There it stood, on the kitchen mantel. She pointed right at it. They hated it worse than most anything in the world.

"I'm all right," said Jehosophat; and

"I'm not sick," protested Marmaduke; and

"Pain's all gone," cried Hepzebiah.

It was funny how the sight of that bottle frightened the three little pains away.

Mother smiled. It was a funny smile. Then she said:

"Now, on with your things!"

Jehosophat sat on the floor and pulled on his new rubber boots, which reached almost to his waist. On the stool sat Marmaduke, putting on his, and Mother helped little Hepzebiah with her wee little ones.

Over Jehosophat's head went a red sweater, over Marmaduke's a green, and over Hepzebiah's curls one of blue. Then wristlets and mittens and coats and caps, and out into the deep white snow they tramped.

"Forward march!" said a voice.

They looked. It was the Toyman.

"The enemy is about to attack," he explained sternly.

"Where's the enemy?"

"You can't see them. But they're advancing fast. Up with the fort. Double quick!"

So at double quick they marched to the barnyard, and began work with their shovels.

My! how they dug! Fast flew the snow. And the Toyman packed it down hard, and shaped it into the walls of a big strong fort.

It was odd, too, how the Toyman could find time to help. For he had lots of work to do. But then the enemy was coming!

Rover and Brownie and Wienerwurst scampered around in the snow. They were not of much help. All they did was to bark - bark - bark.

"Hush!" commanded the Toyman. "We must keep quiet so the enemy won't know where we are."

So they dug and they dug and packed the snow hard. Soon the walls were as high as Jehosophat's shoulders, and the fort was all ready.

The Toyman stopped and said:

"Now for the ammunition."

"What's ammunition?'

"Watch."

The Toyman took a handful of snow and crushed it hard between both hands. When he had finished he opened his fingers. In his palm was a round white ball. Then another he made and another. And the three little soldiers, Jehosophat, Marmaduke, and Hepzebiah, made lots too. They piled them in the corner of the fort, until they had a heap like the iron balls around the cannon in the town park.

"Now," commanded the Toyman. "March to the barracks and get warm" (he pointed at the house). "I'll watch and call when the enemy comes."

Into the house they went, and dried their mittens and warmed their hands. And each had a cup of nice warm milk.

After a while there was a loud knock at the door, and the sound of a horn.

Mother opened the door a little way.

The horn sounded again. Then the voice spoke loudly:

"Fall in," it said. "*The enemy comes!*"

Quickly the three little soldiers put on their mittens and caps, and buttoned their coats, and hurried to the fort.

They looked around. They could not see anybody with a horn. And the Toyman was gone.

Over the walls of the fort they peeked.

There stood six soldiers staring at them. The six soldiers stood very still. They were all white, but their eyes were black like pieces of coal, and they stared hard at the three little soldiers within the fort. Over their shoulders were six long round things.

"Guns," said Jehosophat.

They looked around for the Toyman. He did not come. Their hearts beat fast.

"We're not afraid," shouted Jehosophat at the white soldiers. "Come on, you enemy!"

With that they heard a sound far off.

Rat-a-tat-tat. Rat-a-tat-tat. Rat-a-tat-tat.

"What's that?" cried the smallest little soldier. And Captain Jehosophat answered:

"Drums, drums,

"The enemy comes!"

Then he laughed. He had made a rhyme without thinking anything about it.

But he stopped laughing. It was no time for play. There was hard work ahead. Those six white soldiers in front of the fort were ready to attack. And there were more coming.

"Load!" he commanded.

Each little soldier took up a snowball.

Rat-a-tat-tat. Rat-a-tat-tat. Rat-a-tat-tat.

The drums sounded nearer now.

Rat-a-tat-tat. Rat-a-tat-tat. Rat-a-tat-tat.

Around the house came the sound of the drum.

Over the walls of the fort they peeked - very carefully.

There was a man marching. He looked something like the Toyman. But could it be? No, for he was so changed. The man had a horn around his neck, and a feather in his hat, and his face was stern. He was whistling "Yankee Doodle." It sounded like a fife, and all the time he was beating the drum with all his might.

Rat-a-tat-tat. Rat-a-tat-tat. Rat-a-tat-tat.

On through the snow the Tall Enemy marched. He reached the six white soldiers who stood so still, with their guns over their shoulders.

He stopped and called out to the three little soldiers in the fort in a loud voice:

"SURRENDER OR WE ATTACK!"

"*Never*!" was the brave answer of Captain Jehosophat.

"*Fire*!" he commanded.

Then he let a snowball fly.

He hit the Tall Enemy right in the face.

Then Marmaduke let another snowball fly.

That hit one of the white soldiers and knocked his black eye out.

And Hepzebiah threw her snowball. She tried very hard. But it didn't go very far and didn't do any damage.

Jehosophat looked worried at that. He couldn't depend

Robert Gordon Anderson

on Hepzebiah at all. That left but two of them - against so many - and on came the Tall Enemy with the feather in his cap, still beating his drum.

Rat-a-tat-tat. Rat-a-tat-tat. Rat-a-tat-tat.

The little soldiers must fight bravely now.

Fast flew the snowballs.

He was very near.

Then Marmaduke picked up the last snowball. He took good aim for it was the last of their ammunition. Then he let it fly. It hit the Tall Enemy Man right over his heart.

He fell in the snow.

"You've done for me!" he called in a weak voice.

Then the three little soldiers shouted and ran out of the fort.

There in the snow lay the dying enemy.

"You've won," he said in a sad voice. "I surrender."

"Hurrah, we've won!" they shouted. Then they stopped. They felt very sorry for the enemy, for after all he had been very brave.

They bent over him.

Then something happened. All of a sudden the enemy seized the three little soldiers in his arms.

And he laughed! Yes, laughed.

And hugged them all at once.

And the three little soldiers laughed happily too. For the Tall Enemy had been the Toyman all the time and the six silent soldiers were only made of snow.

Behind his heels they trudged into the house. But the Toyman had to carry the littlest soldier in his arms. She was very cold and very tired.

But the three happy children ate a very good dinner and a very good supper too, that day, for they were very hungry. And they had earned it after the brave fight in the fort.

"Ting-ting." He's always on time, that Little Clock. So Good-night!

Robert Gordon Anderson

FOURTEENTH NIGHT

THE SLEIGH AND THE TINY REINDEER

Marmaduke had played too long in the snow.

He was very wet.

He was very cold.

And he felt very funny and hot all over.

"Mother, my throat's got a rubber ball stuck in it," he said.

Mother looked at it.

"No, dear, there's no rubber ball there, but your throat's all swollen and there are little spots in it. You mustn't get up today."

Marmaduke lay very still for a while. Soon he heard sleigh-bells tinkling past the window, then far down the road. Father had hitched Teddy, the buckskin horse, to the big sleigh and was going for the Doctor.

Away ticked the clock. After a while-a long time it seemed - Marmaduke heard the sleigh-bells again, at first far off, then coming nearer and nearer, until they jingled before the porch - then stopped. He heard voices and the sound of feet upon the porch, shaking off the snow.

The door opened and into the bedroom came the Doctor. He had a face all rosy from the cold. His eyes were black and so sharp that they looked right through Marmaduke. But they were kind eyes and his voice had a pleasant chuckle in it.

The Doctor came and sat on the edge of the bed.

"Well, well! How's my little soldier? Wounded in the battle or just playing possum?"

Then Marmaduke opened his eyes.

After the Doctor had talked a while about lots of different things, before Marmaduke knew it, there was something like a spoon or a shoe-horn in his throat and the Doctor was telling him to say "Ah!"

"This isn't school," thought Marmaduke, "why does he make me say that?"

But he forgot to be frightened, for the Doctor was saying so many funny things all the time.

Then he opened his black bag. It was full of little bottles, packed neatly in rows. Marmaduke wished he would forget and leave it behind. It would be fine to play with.

Mother brought two glasses and the Doctor poured some drops from one bottle into a glass, then from another bottle into another glass. And he said something to Mother in a low voice - Marmaduke could not hear what it was - then he patted the little soldier on the head and said good-bye.

Again the sleigh-bells sounded and away he drove.

But the sleigh-bells never stopped. They kept sounding all the night, long after Teddy was back in his stall and the big sleigh was in the shed. You see Marmaduke was very sick and "out of his head."

Seven days passed and seven nights. He began to feel better, but he was very lonely, for Jehosophat and Hepzebiah had gone to Uncle Roger's to stay while he was sick.

Very small he felt in the big bed in the front room, and very, very lonely. He looked out of the window at the big elms. They were covered with white snow like fur. There were many trees standing in rows. The path between them looked like a white road leading up over the hill to the sky.

He wished he had someone to talk to.

Just then he heard a noise at the door.

"Tap, tap, tap"

It opened just a little.

"Who's there?" said Marmaduke.

The door opened wider. And he saw the Toyman's kind face.

"Hello, little soldier."

"'Llo, Toyman," replied the little boy, and his voice sounded very small and very weak.

The Toyman sat by the bed a while. Then he got up and stirred the fire. Showers of pretty gold and red sparks scampered up the chimney. After that he spread a paper on the floor, not far from the fire-place.

Then his pockets he searched, those big pockets which Mother said were always like five and ten cent stores, they were so full of things.

Out came some pieces of wood. Out came his knife - that magic knife with the five blades. Marmaduke was always glad when he saw that knife for then something nice was sure to happen.

Up came the big blade and snapped back. And the Toyman began to whittle, whittle away. Sometimes he used the big blade, sometimes the small one.

Marmaduke watched him, all eyes.

And as the Toyman whittled sometimes he whistled, and sometimes he sang a funny song in a funny voice. You see he could make rhymes as well as toys.

And this is what he sang:

THE TOYMAN'S SONG

1

"When a little boy's sick

And stays in bed,
And things feel queer
Inside his head.

2

"He cannot work,
He cannot play;
It's hard to pass
The time away.

3

"Don't make much fuss
An' talk a lot;
No questions ask
'Bout what he's got.

4

"They'll ask him that
When Doctor comes,
So just sit still
Like good, ole chums.

5

"An' take your knife
An' make him toys -
This knife knows what
Will please small boys.

6

"Horses and lions,
An' tops and rings,

An' kites and ships,
An' pretty things.

7

"We'll paint 'em red
An' yeller an' blue.
Work away, ole knife,
He's watchin' you!"

That's a new song and a very nice one, thought Marmaduke, as he watched the Toyman whittling away by the red fire.

The little white slivers and shavings covered the paper now. He couldn't see just what that knife was making. But that was nice, too, for then it would be a surprise. And there's nothing finer in the world than a real, beautiful surprise.

Then his head grew very tired, and his eyes began to droop till they were tight shut and he fell asleep.

The Toyman looked at him and smiled.

"Poor little feller!" he said. Then he closed his knife, and picked up the paper and the shavings and the surprise, and out of the room he tiptoed.

Out to the workshop he went, and opened the door.

On the shelves were brushes of different sizes and cans of paint of all colours.

He took down three of the cans, humming to himself:

"We'll paint 'em red
An' yeller an' blue."

"A little brown would go well too," he added as he
took down another can.

He worked away with his paint brushes until the
surprise was finished. Then he placed it on the work-
table to dry.

The next afternoon there was another tap at the
bedroom door.

But Marmaduke didn't answer. He was taking his
afternoon nap. So the Toyman slipped in and put the
surprise at the foot of the bed. After that he sat by the
fire, watching the little sick soldier. He sat very still,
stirring the embers just once in a while to keep the
room warm.

At last Marmaduke opened his eyes, a little at first,
then wider.

The very first thing that he saw at the bottom of the
bed was a tiny sleigh. The body was bright blue and
the runners were red. And what do you think - in front,
hitched to it, were two tiny brown reindeer with yellow
horns! They looked so much alive that Marmaduke
thought any minute they would start running away -
away over the comforter, out of the window, and up
the snow-covered hill.

The Toyman came over to the bed. Marmaduke curled
his little fingers around his friend's hand. The hand was
brown and hard, but it was a nice hand, Marmaduke
thought.

"We're good ole chums, aren't we?" he said to the Toyman.

"You bet we are," the Toyman answered.

FIFTEENTH NIGHT

JACK FROST AND THE MAN-IN-THE-MOON

Once, twice, thrice nodded Marmaduke's head.

The red flames of the fire kept dancing, dancing all the time. Very bright looked the little sleigh at the foot of the bed, very brave the tiny reindeer.

But look! Something moved - just a little.

The "nigh" little reindeer was stamping his foot and tossing his antlers.

And the other little reindeer tossed his horns and stamped his foot too.

On their backs the sleigh-bells jingled, merrily like fairy bells.

The red and blue sleigh moved a little - just a little.

It began to slide slowly, over the comforter.

Marmaduke was worried. He didn't want the pretty sleigh and the reindeer to run away. He might never see them again.

"Wait!" he shouted.

"Whoa - you villains!" It was a strange little voice that ordered the reindeer.

The red and blue sleigh stopped short.

Marmaduke rubbed his eyes.

The strange little voice spoke again.

"Jump in," it said.

And there in the front seat of the toy sleigh sat a funny little chap, about as big as the Toyman's thumb - no bigger. He wore a pointed cap that shone like tinsel on a Christmas tree. He wore a white coat that sparkled too.

"Who are you?" asked the little sick boy. "That's *my* sleigh. You shan't run off with it."

And the funny voice under the white cap answered.

"Jump in, then, and take a ride."

"Tell me who you are, first," Marmaduke insisted.

"My name's Jack."

"Jack what?"

"Jack Frost - you ought to know *that*!"

Tinkle, tinkle went the bells The reindeer lifted their hoofs higher and pawed at the comforter. They shook their antlers impatiently. The little driver jumped up and down in the seat as if he were sitting on pins and needles.

More worried than ever was Marmaduke.

"How can I get in that sleigh?" he asked the imp of a stranger. "I'm too big."

The little chap only chuckled. It was a very mischievous chuckle. Then he said:

"Take a good look at yourself."

Marmaduke did.

My, how he had shrunk! He was no bigger than a brownie, no bigger himself than the Toyman's thumb.

"How did that happen?" he said,

"Oh, the dream fairy did that," said Jack. "She likes to play tricks on people. It's lots of fun. But shake a leg, shake a leg!"

With that he shook the reins himself, and the bells jingled again, and the reindeer grew more eager every second, snorting impatiently.

Once more Marmaduke looked down at himself. No, his eyes had made no mistake. He was small enough now to sit on that little red seat with the tiny driver.

So he popped out from the covers. The folds of the blanket looked as big as mountains, the lumps of the comforter as high as the hills. Over them he scrambled and he sprawled till he reached the little red and blue sleigh.

Then he jumped in.

The driver could be very impudent, but he took good care of Marmaduke just the same, for the boy had been very sick and might catch cold. So Jack pulled the white robe over his passenger's knees, and tucked him in all snug and warm.

"Gee-up, gee-up!" he called to the tiny reindeer.

Marmaduke was frightened. What a horrible crash there would be when they slid from the high bed to the floor.

But nothing like that happened at all. Away off the bed, over the bright rag carpet, and past the red fire, safely and swiftly they trotted. Below the window they paused. Pretty silver ferns and trees covered the panes and sparkled in the firelight. The window was closed, but that did not matter at all.

"Up with you!" yelled Jack Frost.

Slowly, as if by magic, up went the window sash! Over the sill galloped the reindeer. And after them ran the toy sleigh with Jack Frost and Marmaduke on the red seat.

Over the porch, too, they went.

Then something did happen.

"Now look at yourself," said Jack Frost, cracking

Robert Gordon Anderson

his whip.

Marmaduke did not hear him at first. He was admiring that whip. It was only a long icicle, and all Jack had to do was to touch the reindeer with its point to make them run faster and faster.

"Look at yourself," he repeated.

Marmaduke obeyed.

"Why, I'm as big as I used to be!"

Jack laughed and replied:

"The dream fairy does love to play tricks on folks!"

Yes, the sleigh had grown as large as his father's sleigh; the reindeer as big as Teddy, the buckskin horse. The tossing horns were as high as the reindeer's in the Zoo, and Jack Frost was as big as Jehosophat now.

"I'm sorry that Jehosophat and Hepzebiah are not along," said Marmaduke to himself, "they're going to miss some fun"

He looked ahead through the trees Up over the hill the snow path stretched - up to the dark blue sky and the stars. Millions of them there were and they were all twinkle-winking at him. And the Old Man-in-the-Moon, just over the hill, kept winking at him too.

Jack Frost turned to Marmaduke.

"Where would you like to go *most*?"

Marmaduke didn't need to think, he had his answer all ready.

"I'd like to visit the Old Man-in-the Moon."

"It's a bit of a drive," replied Jack, "but Old Yellow Horns and Prancing Hoof are fast goers. Gee-up! Gee-up!" he shouted at them, touching their flanks with the icicle whip. So fast they went they scarcely seemed to touch the snow, and on up the hill they rode towards the laughing Man-in-the-Moon.

Then suddenly there came such a barking, a yelping, a neighing, a mooing, a clucking, a gobbling, a squealing, a squawling, as you never heard before.

Around jerked Marmaduke's head.

There, behind the sleigh, running and leaping and paddling and waddling and frisking and scampering came a strange procession. There were Rover and Brownie and little Wienerwurst, Teddy and Methusaleh and all the horses, Primrose, Daisy, Buttercup, Black-Eyed Susan and all the cows. He could see *their* tongues hanging out - it was so hard to keep up with the dogs and the horses.

"Moo - moo, slow - slow!" called the poor cows.

And behind them ambled the sheep and the curley-tailed pigs; waddled the ducks and the geese; Miss Crosspatch, the Guinea Hen, and Mr. Stuckup, the turkey; and, at the very end, all of the White Wyandottes, the fathers and the mothers, and the little yellow children, and their grandfathers and grandmothers, and all their uncles and aunts, and their

Robert Gordon Anderson

cousins, first, second, and third - every last one of them.

My - what a fuss and a clatter they made!

There was a long long line of them, stretching down the hill and down the white road over the snow.

Marmaduke laughed and exclaimed to Jack Frost:

"Why, they look just like the procession of the animals when they came out of the Ark."

"Yes, I remember them," replied Jack. "And Old Noah too. I used to pinch their ears and pull their tails o' nights."

Marmaduke looked surprised.

"You! Why, that was *hundreds* of years ago! You can't be as old as all that."

But Jack only smiled a superior smile

"Sure I am. Why I'm as old as the world!"

"Old as that Man-in-the-Moon?" continued Marmaduke, and the odd little fellow replied:

"Just as old."

Marmaduke looked up at the moon sailing far above them. And the old man, sitting there on the moon-mountain, nodded as much as to say that Jack was quite right.

Now the sleigh reached the top of the hill just where it touches the sky.

Surely there they would stop.

But no -

"This sleigh can run on air just as well as on snow," the odd little driver explained.

Another touch of the icicle whip, a jingle of bells, a snort from the reindeer, and they were off - off through the air towards the sailing moon.

Marmaduke was so interested in looking up that he didn't see little Wienerwurst run ahead of all the animals. That doggie beat them all to the top of the hill. And when he came to the top he just jumped out in the air and landed safe on the runner of the sleigh, and curled up there and hid and didn't make any noise.

It was very clear high up in the air, and Marmaduke looked down.

The houses had shrivelled all up. As small as Wienerwurst's own little house they seemed. And the trees were as small as plants in the garden.

He looked down again. The earth was far below them.

By the white steeple of the church they flew. In the steeple was a little window. The bell-rope hung out. Jack jerked it as they went past.

"Ding, dong -
Something's wrong."

So spoke the deep voice of the old bell. He was a hundred years old, and such strange things had never happened in his life before.

And the minister threw up his window and stuck his head out. And the minister's wife stuck her head, in her nightcap, out of the window, too. And the sexton ran out in the snow, in his shirt-tail, to see what was the matter.

And all the other people, in the farmhouses and in the town houses, threw up their windows or ran out of doors to see where the fire was.

Then, after looking all around the houses and barns and the haystacks, they looked up at the sky and saw Marmaduke in the sleigh, racing towards the moon

They were very funny, like little toy people, all looking up and pointing at the sky and all shouting at once.

But Marmaduke didn't care - he was having the time of his life!

Then a still stranger and funnier sight he saw, - all the animals on the top of the hill - the horses, the dogs, the cows, the sheep, the pigs, the ducks, the geese, the turkeys, and the White Wyandottes, all sitting on their haunches and barking or neighing or howling or squawking at Marmaduke, as on - up and up - he went, a-sailing through the sky.

But he missed his little pet doggie. Where *could* he be?

He was worried about that until all of a sudden he heard a little bark and looked behind, and there on the red runner, hanging on for dear life, was little Wienerwurst. Marmaduke reached down, and picked him up by the scruff of his neck, and set him on his lap, under the robe, so that he wouldn't catch cold.

So Wienerwurst too had the time of his life, and his little pink tongue hung out in delight as they raced toward the moon.

They hadn't gone more than a hundred miles or so, when something strange floated past them - a cloud all puffy and soft and white, like the floating islands in the puddings Mother makes.

The reindeer nearly ran into it. That would have been too bad, for the sleigh would have torn it in two. And as they passed, Marmaduke saw little baby angels lying there, curled up in the cloud, fast asleep, with their wings folded.

A whole fleet of the clouds passed by and there was only clear air ahead of them, they thought, but no!

"Bang." They had bunked into something high up in the sky.

"Very careless," said Jack Frost, as he pulled on the reins.

It was very bright, and Marmaduke blinked hard.

Ahead of them lay another island, but this one was round and flat and shiny like a gold shield, with a little hill in the centre. And there upon the hill sat a jolly old man, round and fat, with a pipe in his mouth and a sack on his back.

Robert Gordon Anderson

"Hello, old Top!" said Jack Frost.

"Good evening, you mischief-maker," replied the Man-in-the-Moon. "What are you up to now?"

"Oh, I've brought one of the little earth children to see you. This is Marmaduke Green. He's been sick, so I thought I'd give him a ride."

"Oh, ho! That's it. You *do* do someone a good turn now and then, after all."

Then the old man turned to Marmaduke.

"Howdy," he said, "I hope you'll get better very soon."

"Thank you," replied Marmaduke politely. He was so well brought up that he didn't forget his manners, even up high in the sky.

"Well, here's something to play with when you get back to earth," said the Old Man-in-the-Moon. And he reached his hand inside the sack on his back, and pulled out a fistful of bright gold pennies - oh, such a lot of them!

Marmaduke reached for them. But alas! he was in too much of a hurry, and they spilled out of his hand and rolled right over the edge of the moon. Down, down, down, through the sky they dropped, past the stars and the clouds, down, down, down to the earth.

There were all the animals still, on the top of the hill, looking up at the moon. And one of the bright pennies landed on Black-eyed Susan's nose. She was a timid old cow and she was startled. And she was still more frightened at the howling, the barking, the squawking, which the animals set up, one and all.

So frightened was she that she jumped. So hard did she jump that she leaped way over the hill and over the clouds and the stars.

"There's that critter again," complained the Man-in-the-Moon.

On, with her tail spread out behind her, and her legs sprawling in the sky, came old Black-eyed Susan, straight towards them. Jack Frost and Marmaduke jumped back; the Old Man-in-the-Moon moved a little too. They were afraid she would land on their toes.

But she didn't.

"She's still pretty chipper," observed the old man. "That's a great jump. Most beats the record"

So it did, for she sailed right over them, coming down on the other side of the moon, hitting one poor little star on the way with her hoof, and putting out its light entirely.

And down, down old Susan fell till she hit the earth and lay there, panting and mooing so loud that the people on earth thought it was thunder, and shut their windows tight for fear of the rain.

"Well!" said the Old Man-in-the-Moon, blowing clouds of smoke from his pipe, "that's over. Now here's some more pennies. Be careful this time," he warned him.

And from his sack he drew forth another great handful of gold pennies. How they did shine! But as Marmaduke reached for them, Jack Frost jiggled his elbow with his icicle whip - and again they rolled over the edge of the moon.

And again Marmaduke was too eager. He ran after them, and Wienerwurst ran too, and when they reached the edge they couldn't stop themselves at all.

They were falling, down, down through the sky. A hundred somersaults they turned. Marmaduke tried to hold on to a cloud, but his hands went right through it. He tried to hold on to the stars, but he missed every one.

Then suddenly - bang went his head against the church steeple - - - and all the stars danced - - - - - - - - - - - - -

Then he woke.

He looked around. Why-he was sitting up in the bed, his very own bed, by the red fire!

It was just a trick of the dream fairy's, after all.

But it was all right, for at the foot of the bed rested the little red and blue sleigh and the tiny reindeer, just as still as still could be.

And at the side of the bed stood Father and Mother - and the Toyman.

They seemed very happy.

SIXTEENTH NIGHT

SLOSHIN'

Of course Marmaduke grew well again, and back from Uncle Roger's came Jehosophat and Hepzebiah. They came back in the old creaking buckboard with Methuselah the old, old white horse, and the Toyman.

No sooner had they jumped to the ground than Marmaduke asked, very proudly:

"Where do you think *I've* been?"

"You've been sick."

Marmaduke shook his head.

"That's not what I mean," he said. "I've been to see the Old Man-in-the-Moon."

"*Now* you're telling *stories*" jeered Jehosophat. "You've just been in *bed* all the time."

"I'm *not* telling any stories," said his brother stoutly. "I tell you, I *have* been to visit the Old Man-in-the-Moon."

But Jehosophat wouldn't believe him.

Robert Gordon Anderson

"That's a *whopper*," said he.

Marmaduke turned to his friend, the Toyman.

"I *have* been there, haven't I?"

"Where?" said the Toyman.

"To see the Old Man-in-the-Moon."

"Of course you have," his good old chum replied, "and a heap of wonderful things you saw."

The Toyman never laughed at the wonderful things they had done, nor at the marvellous things they had seen - no never, for he understood little children.

Now Jehosophat *had* to believe him. He asked lots of questions, while Hepzebiah listened, her eyes growing as round as big peppermint drops.

So Marmaduke showed them the little red and blue sleigh, and told them all about the little driver, Jack Frost. And he didn't forget about old Black-eyed Susan's great jump, nor the gold pennies, either.

Jehosophat felt just a little jealous. Perhaps that is why he was naughty that day.

And this is how it all happened:

It was in the afternoon. Jehosophat was coming home from the schoolhouse, which was up the road about a mile, a long way from the White-House-with-the-Green-Blinds where the three happy children lived.

With him walked four of his friends - Sophy Soapstone and Sammy Soapstone, who lived on the farm by the Old Canal; Lizzie Fizzletree, who lived on the turnpike; and Fatty Hamm, who lived by the river road.

Sammy Soapstone had blue eyes and tow hair which stood up straight on his head. It was as stiff as the curry comb with which the Toyman brushed the horses. Sophy Soapstone had blue eyes, too, and two neat little pigtails down her back.

But Lizzie Fizzletree had black eyes and hair that stuck out in all directions. She had more safety-pins on her dress than a neat little girl should ever have. And her stockings were forever coming down.

Fatty Hamm was so round and so plump that he looked as if he had pillows under his clothes. And though he was only twelve he had two chins. Every once in a while he would eat so much that a button would pop off.

He was eating apples now.

One, two, three, four, five, he ate. He did not offer one to his friends, *not even the core*!

Another apple he took. That made six!

Pop went a button and - splash - it landed in a puddle of brown water.

For three days it had rained, washing the white snow away. The ruts in the road were full of these puddles, nice and brown and inviting.

Robert Gordon Anderson

Sammy's eyes and Jehosophat's eyes followed the button as it landed in the water, making little rings which grew larger all the time.

"Let's slosh," said Sammy.

"Let's!" cried Lizzie Fizzletree, "it's lots of fun, sloshin'."

Into a big puddle marched Sammy Soapstone, and after him marched Lizzie and Sophy, and at the end of the procession waddled Fatty.

"Slop, slosh, slop, slosh," they went through puddle after puddle.

Glorious fun it was. Showers of spray flew all over the road.

But Jehosophat walked on ahead in the middle of the road. Hadn't his mother told him, particularly, *not* to get his feet wet?

"Come on in, it's fine!" they all shouted at Jehosophat.

"Aw, come on!" Sammy Soapstone repeated, and Fatty called:

"'Fraidcat!"

At that Jehosophat turned around. He just couldn't stand being called "'fraidcat."

So *slosh, slosh*, into the biggest brown puddle he could find he went.

Slosh, slop, slop, slosh!

Over his rubber tops went the water. Fine and cool it felt.

Splash went the water over the road. And he kicked it over Fatty till the round fat legs were drenched too.

Then all the boys bent over the puddle, and scooped up great handfuls of water, and threw them over each other.

It was a great battle. And when it was finished and they were soaked to the skin, they splashed up the road, shouting and singing.

I guess they went into every last puddle between the schoolhouse and the White-House-with-the-Green-Blinds by the side of the road.

They had reached it now.

All-of-a-sudden Jehosophat felt very funny near the pit of his stomach. Something was sure to happen now.

In front of the house marched Mr. Stuckup, the Turkey. His chest was stuck out and his tail feathers were spread out too, like a great big fan. He was having a lovely parade all by himself.

"Rubber, rubber, rubber," he gobbled.

Jehosophat looked down at his feet. He felt guilty - but he thought it was very mean of Mr. Stuckup to call attention to his wet rubbers that way.

"Keep quiet," Jehosophat shouted. "You don't need to *tell* on me!"

"Rubber, rubber, rubber," gobbled Mr. Stuckup just the same.

Jehosophat kicked at him with his wet feet, and tried to grab the fat red nose that hung down over the turkey's beak.

At that old Mr. Stuckup's feathers ruffled in anger, and he hurried off, still gobbling "rubber, rubber, rubber," as loud as he could.

Around the house sneaked Jehosophat, trying hard not to be seen.

Half-way to the back door, who should he meet but a procession of the Foolish White Geese.

By this time Jehosophat was not only wet clear through, he was angry clear through too, so he kicked at them.

They stretched out their long white necks and called:

"Hiss! Hiss! Hisssssssss!!"

They might be very foolish, these White Geese, but they were sensible enough to know that Jehosophat ought to have been ashamed of himself that afternoon.

To make matters worse, the sun was shining now. He sparkled so brightly on the Gold Rooster on the top of the barn, that Father Wyandotte flapped his wings and cried to all the world:

"Look, look, look, look! You're going to get it - hurroo!"

And all the White Wyandottes took up the cry:

"Cut, cut, cut, cut, cut - you'll get it."

Jehosophat wished he were as small as Hop-o'-my-Thumb, so that he could creep through the keyhole and never be seen at all.

But he had one friend left - little Wienerwurst, who frisked up to him just then, wagging his tail. He didn't scold Jehosophat at all, partly because he was so often up to mischief himself. And then little Wienerwurst always stuck by his friends anyway.

For a while nothing more happened, and Jehosophat tiptoed in at the back door. Mother was nowhere to be seen, so over the floor he sneaked.

At every step the water oozed out and *slop, splosh, slop, splosh*, still went his shoes.

But he reached his room safely, then quickly he rummaged in the drawers of the bureau.

Quiet as a mouse he took off his wet clothes, and put them in the darkest corner of the big closet. Quiet as a mouse he drew on the clean dry ones.

But someone was calling:

"Jehosophat - *Je-hos'-o-phat*!"

No answer made he.

Robert Gordon Anderson

"Jehosophat - *Je-hos'-o-phat*!"

No longer could he hide. So, making his face look as bold and as innocent as possible, he walked into the dining-room.

But somehow, though he tried to look innocent, I guess he really looked guilty.

"Jehosophat Green, what *have* you been doing?" asked Mother. Her eyes were almost always kind but they were a little stern just then.

Jehosophat tried another look on his face, for you can try different looks on your face just as you try different hats on your head. This time he tried the one that folks call "unconcern," a look as if he had no troubles at all, as if he had nothing to hide.

"Aw, just playin'," he answered his mother.

Then his mother asked a very strange question:

"Where's the party?"

Jehosophat *was* surprised. "Party" sounded fine.

"What party, Mother?" he asked.

"I don't know," his mother replied. "I just thought you were dressed up for one."

And he looked down at his clean suit and his Sunday best shoes. And from out the corner of his eye he saw wet places on the floor and muddy tracks, about as big as his feet.

No answer now had Jehosophat. He guessed he would go into the parlour. So he sat down at the marble-topped table, and looked at the picture book which Uncle Roger had given him. It was full of great white ships sailing the blue sea.

For a moment he almost forgot all his troubles, so interested was he in looking at those great ships and their sails and all the wonderful fish.

Then suddenly he remembered.

He looked out through the door into the dining-room.

Mother wasn't saying anything. She was just busy. That was all.

But had she forgotten?

Somehow Jehosophat did not like the sad look on her face.

He went and shut the door. He thought he would feel more comfortable if he couldn't see Mother's eyes. Then he sat down to look at the picture book again. But he felt more miserable than ever.

Bang! he shut the book too. It was very strange. The things that usually made him so happy weren't any fun at all just then.

Then he looked up at the mantel.

Above it hung a great picture. There was a man in a cocked hat. He had on a fine uniform and he rode a tall white horse. Jehosophat knew very well who that was.

It would be *his* birthday tomorrow - George Washington's birthday. The teacher had told them all about it that very afternoon.

She had told them a story, too, about a hatchet and a cherry tree - and - a lie!

The man on the horse looked down from the picture. The eyes were very stern.

A lie!

Yes, that was just what he had told to Mother. He had told a lie, and acted a lie.

Though there was no one else in the room but the great man in the big picture, Jehosophat's cheeks grew very red. A lump came into his throat.

Now he never could be president nor have a sword - and ride a big white horse - and call "Forward March" to the whole army. No - never!

To the window he went, and pressed his nose against the pane. The clouds were grey. It all seemed very dark and not at all cheerful as the world ought to be.

Once more he looked up at the picture.

And as he looked at the eyes of the man in the picture, they told him to do something.

He decided to do it. And as soon as he decided he felt better - not *all* better - but better.

And out into the dining-room he marched. He had to

close his fists tight, for it is very hard sometimes to tell people you've done wrong to them, especially if they are people you love.

"Mother," he said - not very loud.

She looked up.

"Yes?"

"Mother - I -"

He stopped. Mother looked up. She saw his lip tremble a little and wanted to take him in her arms. But she didn't just then. He must tell what he had to tell, first.

"Mother - I told a lie - I got my feet wet - sloshin' - and I said I was playin' when I changed my clothes - an' I'm sorry an' - an' - I'll never do it again."

Then Mother did take him in her arms and she kissed him and hugged him too.

"Well - I love my little boy all the more for this. It was very wrong to disobey, worse still to tell a lie. But it was hard to tell me your own self about it and you were brave."

So she kissed him. And her eyes weren't sad any more.

SEVENTEENTH NIGHT

THE CIRCUS COMES TO TOWN

Mother Green and Father Green were fast asleep in the White-House-with-the-Green-Blinds. The Toyman was fast asleep too. Rover and Brownie and Wienerwurst lay curled up in their kennels, with their eyes tight shut. On their poles in *their* house all the White Wyandottes perched like feathery balls, their heads sunk low on their breasts. On the roof cuddled the pretty pigeons, all pink and grey and white. In the barn Teddy, and Hal, and Methuselah, and Black-eyed Susan, and all the four-footed friends of the three happy children, rested from the cares of the day. Hepzebiah never stirred in her crib, and Jehosophat lay dreaming of something very pleasant.

But the crickets, and the katydids, the scampering mice, and the big-eyed owls, and the little stars, snapping their tiny fingers of light up in the sky, and Marmaduke - *they* were awake.

He had played very hard that day and he had leg-ache. Mother had rubbed it till it felt better and he fell asleep, but now it began to hurt again and he woke up. The Little-Clock-with-the-Wise-Face-on-the-Mantel struck, not seven times but four. It was long past midnight - *it was four o 'clock in the morning*!

But Marmaduke didn't call his mother. He thought that it would be too bad to wake her up from that nice sleep. So he just tried to rub his leg himself.

It was then that he heard that far-off noise like a rumble of thunder. But it wasn't thunder. It was something rolling over the bridge down the road.

Marmaduke sat up in bed and looked out of the window into the dark shadows of the trees.

There was another rumble, and another and another. There must be, oh, so many wagons rolling by in the night. Then he heard the sound of horses' hoofs on the road, the clank of rings and iron trace chains.

He rubbed his eyes this time and looked hard out into the darkness.

Yes, he could see the tops of the big wagons, moving slowly past, under the trees and over the road.

It was a strange procession and he just had to jump out of bed, forgetting all about his leg-ache. He ran to the window, pressing his little turned-up nose against the panes.

Though it was dark still it must have been near morning. The moon was just going down behind the Church-with-the-Long-White-Finger, that finger which always kept pointing at the sky. The Old Man-in-the-Moon looked very tired and peaked after sitting up so late.

There were so many of the wagons and so many horses. They must stretch way back to the

Robert Gordon Anderson

school-house, and miles and miles beyond that, Marmaduke thought.

The horses seemed very tired, for they plodded along slowly in the dark, and the drivers almost fell asleep, nodding on their seats. They looked just like black shadows.

Under the axles of the wagons were lanterns, swinging a little and throwing circles of light on the road.

Now and then one of the drivers spoke roughly to the horses. And sometimes Marmaduke heard strange noises like the sleepy growls of wild animals. Perhaps they were in those wagons!

Then Marmaduke laughed. He knew what it was. They were circus wagons! The circus was coming to town! The Toyman had told him all about it, that very day.

Once, one of the animals roared and the others answered back. Their noise was louder than the rumble of the wagon-wheels on the bridge. Marmaduke was frightened. But the roaring stopped, and all he could hear was the noise of all those wheels on their way up the road by the river.

Then the last wagon passed and Marmaduke went back to bed and fell asleep.

But the long procession rolled on and on till it reached the church. There was a large field nearby. Into it the wagons turned and all the horses were unhitched.

Then the cooks started fires in the stoves on the cook-wagons, and all the strange men and women had coffee. And then, just as the Sun was coming up and the night was all gone, they went to work.

Up in the centre of the field they raised three tall poles. They were almost as high as the Long White Finger of the Church. They drove many stakes into the ground. And around the tall poles they stretched almost as many ropes as there are on a ship.

Then they unrolled the white canvas and, when the Sun was just a little way up in the sky and the morning was all nice and shiny and bright, the great white tents were ready for the circus.

Back in the White-House-with-the-Green-Blinds, Marmaduke was eating his oatmeal. He asked a question that he very often asked:

"What do you think *I* saw?"

"Another dream?" said Jehosophat.

"No, it was *real*," replied Marmaduke. "I saw a lot of wagons, hundreds 'n thousands, in a big line miles long. And there were wild animals in the wagons."

"I'll bet that was a *dream*," his big brother insisted, but the Toyman said:

"No, it wasn't a dream, it was the circus coming to town."

Then Father spoke up:

"That's so, I most forgot."

He looked at the Toyman:

"Frank," he said, "I've got to go over to the Miller farm to buy some yearling steers. You'll have to take the youngsters to that circus."

The Toyman didn't seem worried about that. He looked just "tickled," "like a boy himself," Mother said.

So, after dinner, old Methuselah was hitched up, and away they drove, - the Toyman, Jehosophat, Hepzebiah, and Marmaduke, with little Wienerwurst, as usual, in back. He was very happy, barking at all the carriages hurrying up the road to the circus.

They came to the field with the big white tents and were just going to turn in, when they heard music way off in the streets of the town.

"Why, I most forgot," said the Toyman to Jehosophat. "There's the circus parade over on Main Street. In the big city they have the parade and the circus all in one big building, but in the country towns they have the parade first in the street, and the performance after, in the tents."

"Tluck, tluck!" he called to Methuselah, and jog, jog, jog, the old horse trotted into town. In Uncle Roger's barn the Toyman unhitched him, and gave him some hay and some oats too, for it was a grand holiday. Then hand-in-hand the Toyman and the three happy children hurried over to Main Street.

So many people were crowded on the sidewalk that the children could hardly see. But Jehosophat ducked under the stomachs of two big fat men and sat on the curb-stone. And the Toyman held Marmaduke on one shoulder and Hepzebiah on the other. He was very strong. From their high perch they could look right over the heads of all the people at that great circus parade.

Hark! They were coming!

First the band. They were dressed in gay uniforms of red and blue, with gold tassels too, and bright brass buttons.

Ahead of them marched the leader of the band - the tall Drum Major. He had on a high fur cap, twice as big as his head. In his hand he swung a long black cane, called a "baton." It had a gold knob on it, bigger than a duck's egg.

He raised the cane and the music began!

Trrat -- trrat -- trrat - trrat - trrat! went the little drums.

Boom -- boom -- boom - boom - boom! went the big bass drum.

hum -

hum -

hum -

Hum -

hum - hum!

Robert Gordon Anderson

sounded the shiny horns.

ter-loo

ter-loo

ter-loo

Loo-loo-loo

ter-loo-loo!

gaily whistled the little fifes.

Then they all sounded together in a grand crash of music that made all the people happy and excited, and they almost danced on the sidewalk.

And all the time the tall Drum-Major kept twirling that baton with the gold knob on it till Jehosophat's eyes most popped out of his head.

My! how he could twirl it!

But other wonderful things were coming now, marching by very swiftly, - ladies on horses that pranced and danced; cowboys on horses that were livelier still; a giant as tall as the big barber's pole; and a dwarf no higher than that tall giant's knee.

And great grey elephants, all tied together by their trunks and their tails; and zebras like little horses painted with stripes; and cages on wagons, full of funny monkeys, making faces at all the people; and lions and tigers, walking up and down and showing their sharp teeth.

Then something happened!

One of the circus men must have been sleepy that morning, for he hadn't fixed the lock on that cage just tight. And the big tiger felt very mean that day. He snarled and he snarled, and he jumped at the bars of his cage.

Open came the door. Out leaped that wicked tiger right on the street, and the people ran pell mell in all directions.

The two fat men were so frightened that they fell flat on their stomachs. The barber shinnied up his pole, and hung on for dear life to the top. The baker-man tumbled into the watering-trough, and all the rest rushed higgledy-piggledy into the houses and stores.

The Toyman picked up Hepzebiah, Marmaduke, and Jehosophat, hurried them into the candy-store, and shut the door tight.

It was full of beautiful candies, - chocolate creams and peppermint drops, snowy white cocoanut cakes, black and white licorice sticks, and cherry-red lollypops. But the three children never noticed those lovely candies at all. They just looked out of the glass door at that tiger, walking up and down the street, a-showing his teeth and a-swishing his tail.

The tiger looked at all the people behind the windows and doors. They were all shivering in their boots, and he didn't know which one to choose. Then he looked up at the man on the barber-pole, and he was shivering too.

Robert Gordon Anderson

Then all of a sudden the tiger stopped.

"*Girrrrrrrrrrrhhh!*"

He saw the butcher shop.

The door was open. Some nice red pieces of beef hung on the hooks.

He licked his chops and ran into the shop and jumped up at the first piece of beef and ate it all up. He never saw the stout butcher, who was hiding under the chopping block. The butcher's face was usually as red as the beef, but now it was as white as his apron, and his feet were shaking as fast as leaves in the wind.

But just as the tiger was gobbling the last morsel up, down the street galloped a cowboy on a swift horse. He stopped right in front of the butcher shop.

Out went his hand.

In it was a rope all coiled up.

Around his head he twirled it, in great flying loops. Then he let it fly.

And it fell around that wicked tiger's head and neck, just as he was finishing his dinner.

Then the circus men came with big steel forks, and they ran at that tiger, and they tied him all up in that rope very tight, and put him back in the cage on the wagon, while he growled and growled and growled.

So the parade started again and all of the people came

out of their hiding-places, all but the fat men who hurried off home, as soon as they found their breath, and the old ladies who said they guessed they'd go to missionary meeting after all. A circus parade was too heathenish.

Soon it was all over, and the rest of the people hurried off to the field with the big white tents.

And what they saw there we will tell you tomorrow night.

Robert Gordon Anderson

EIGHTEENTH NIGHT

THE JOLLY CLOWN

Marmaduke was lost. There was such a crowd around those tents! He wriggled between lots of pairs of legs, but nowhere could he find the Toyman's.

Near the door of the tent stood a man with a big black moustache, and a silk hat on his head. He was selling tickets. The Toyman went up to him.

"Howdy," said the Toyman.

"Howdy, pardner," replied he.

"I'd like four tickets. Here is the money. One whole ticket and three half tickets too."

The man counted the money and gave him the tickets. Then the Toyman asked:

"Did you see a little boy 'bout this high, with a little yeller dog?"

The man with the big black moustache and the tall silk hat shook his head.

"Sorry I can't oblige you, pardner. I've seen lots of

kiddies but nary a one with a yeller dog."

"Well then," said the Toyman, "will you kindly show these youngsters to their seats while I look for that little lost boy and his dog?"

"Certainly, be most pleased," was the answer, for all circus men are very polite on Circus Day.

So the man with the black moustache and the tall silk hat called a man in a red cap. Jehosophat took Hepzebiah by the hand, and the man in the red cap led them into the big tent. He showed them their seats, and they sat down in the very front row.

Outside, the Toyman kept looking, looking everywhere. There was no sign of Marmaduke's tow head nor of little yellow Wienerwurst.

They were on the other side of the tent, outside too, mixed up with men and women they didn't know, and hundreds of boys and girls. They could see other men too, with striped shirts and loud voices, standing in small houses. And the small houses looked just like little stores, and on the counters were good things to eat, - popcorn, peanuts, cracker jack, and something cool in glasses, like lemonade but coloured like strawberries. Loud did the men shout, trying to sell those good things to everybody who came near.

But Marmaduke couldn't buy even *one* peanut. He didn't have any money. How was he ever going to get into that circus!

Oh, where was the Toyman?

But he didn't cry. You know he didn't. He just shut his teeth hard, and winked and winked.

At last Wienerwurst gave a little bark. He saw a little hole, and Wienerwurst always liked little holes. It was under the tent and just his size. Right into it he crawled. All Marmaduke could see of his doggie now was his little tail like a sausage. The rest of him was under the tent. Thump-thump-thump went the tail. And Marmaduke knew it must be pretty nice inside.

Then the tail, too, disappeared. So down on his stomach went the little boy and crawled right in after his doggie.

The tent had several big rooms and he was in one of them. On every side were big cages with iron bars.

"*Girrrrrrrrrrhhh!*" went something in one of the cages.

That wicked runaway tiger!

Marmaduke ran past all the cages very fast until he came to another room. In it were lots of queer funny people.

He heard another voice, not like the runaway tiger's, but one just happy and pleasant, though very deep.

"Well, look who's here!" it said.

That was a funny thing to say, Marmaduke thought, and he looked up.

He had to look up ever so high. There was the tall

giant, sitting on a great big chair. Big were his feet and his legs and his hands, and big were his chin and his nose and his hat. Still he didn't look cross like the giants in the story-books, just nice and kind.

Marmaduke stared up at him and he smiled down at Marmaduke.

It was very hot and the big giant took off his hat to wipe his forehead. He set his hat down. He didn't look where he put it and it went over Marmaduke's head and nearly covered him up. He couldn't see any sunlight. It was all dark inside that hat.

"Let me out," he shouted. And he heard someone say:

"What's in your hat?"

"There *was* a little boy around here," the giant replied. "Maybe I've covered him up."

The giant leaned down and picked up his hat, and took it off the little boy. Very glad was Marmaduke to see the light once more.

The giant bowed low to apologize and the great chair creaked.

"Very careless of me," he said. "A thousand pardons, Sir!"

Marmaduke felt very happy. It was fine to be called "Sir" by a great big giant like that.

Then he felt himself being lifted up, and there he sat on the giant's knee. The giant told him a story and gave him a big ring from his finger. It was so large that Marmaduke could put his whole arm through it.

Then another voice spoke. It was a little tiny voice this time - no bigger than a mouse's squeak or a cricket's "Good-night."

Marmaduke looked down from the giant's knee.

"Hello, little fellow," squeaked the funny little voice.

No, it was not Jack Frost. It was a dwarf, all dressed in a crimson velvet gown, with a gold crown on her head. The top of the crown wasn't even as high as the giant's knee. My, but she *was* little!

Marmaduke was just going to say, "Little, *huh*! I'm as big as *you* are!" But he didn't. That wouldn't have been quite right when all these circus people were so very polite to him.

So all he said was:

"Good-afternoon!"

And the little tiny lady in the crimson gown gave him something too, - a silver button from her dress. Then the giant handed him over to a lady who sat next. A very funny lady was she, for she had a woman's voice and a woman's dress and a woman's hair, too, but on her chin was a long, long beard, just like a man's.

The bearded lady kissed Marmaduke. He didn't like that, she tickled so.

He didn't go very near the one who sat next. Yet *she*

was a very pretty lady with blue eyes and golden hair, but around her arms and neck instead of necklaces were curled up snakes!

"They won't bite, little boy," she said smiling. "Look out for the *snakes in the grass*, but don't mind these. They can't hurt you at all."

With that she handed him some candy.

Marmaduke's hands were so full now, with the candy and the big ring and the silver button, that he didn't know what to do.

Just ahead of him was little Wienerwurst's tail. The very thing! So he put that big ring over that little tail. That felt so funny that Wienerwurst tried to reach his tail and that round shiny thing on it.

Around and around he went in a circle, trying to bite it off. He looked as if his head and tail were tied together. Like a little yellow merry-go-round, whirling so swiftly after itself, was he. All the strange circus people laughed and cheered and the giant clapped his huge hands till they sounded like thunder.

All of a sudden the ring rolled off Wienerwurst's tail, and Marmaduke went scrambling after it. It rolled right near the lady - and all those snakes!

Marmaduke didn't like *that*. He was glad when he heard another voice call out, very cheerily.

"Here it is, Sonny!"

This was a very jolly voice, jollier than any he had

ever heard in the world except the Toyman's.

The man who owned that voice stood before him, such a funny man, in a baggy white suit, with red spots like big red tiddledy winks all over it. He had a pointed cap all red and white too. And his face was all painted white, with long black eyebrows and a wide, wide, red mouth.

This was the way Marmaduke met Tody the Clown.

They had a long talk together and he seemed to understand little boys, just like the Toyman.

"It must be fine to always live in a circus," said Marmaduke. "Wish I did."

"Well, Sonny, when you grow up, maybe you can," replied Tody the Clown.

Marmaduke looked at the wide mouth with its funny smile.

"You're always happy, aren't you?"

Tody nodded and answered:

"Sure - anyway *almost* always."

"Don't you ever feel cross or have any troubles?"

Tody threw back his head at that and laughed way out loud.

"Sure I do," said he. "A heap of troubles, but I just think of all the little girls and boys like you that I've got to make happy. Then I try hard to make 'em laugh and -"

"An' what?"

"Why all my troubles fly away, quick as a wink," laughed Tody. "Yes, just as quick as I do this." And *quicker* than a wink he turned a somersault. He turned a whole lot of somersaults and then he took Marmaduke on his shoulder and galloped around the tent and they had a glorious time.

But the music was sounding out in the big tent just next them - drums and horns and bugles and fifes. The circus would start in a minute now and all the fun would be over.

"Where's your ticket, Sonny?" asked Tody.

"I haven't any," Marmaduke explained. "I've lost the Toyman - and he's got my ticket an' - an' - I can't go in."

"Don't you worry about that. You'll have the *best seat in the whole circus*." And Tody turned another somersault just to make him laugh. Then he looked down at little Wienerwurst.

"But they won't let any doggies in there. We'll just tie him to this pole."

Marmaduke shook his head and tried hard to keep the tears back. Just one little one rolled down his right cheek But that was on the other side of Tody. Maybe Tody saw it anyway, for when Marmaduke said to him, - "Then I can't go in either, my little pet doggie would feel so badly," the jolly Clown answered:

"Well, we'll just have to fix it up some way. Can y' keep him quiet?"

"Quiet as a mouse," answered Marmaduke, "quiet as Mother Robin when she sits on her nest."

And Wienerwurst barked out loud just to show how quiet he could be.

Tody spoke to another man. This one had on a bright red vest, red as Father Robin's. He looked at the boy and the dog. His voice wasn't as pleasant as Tody's nor the giant's, but what he said was all right.

It was just "Sure!" and Marmaduke and Wienerwurst slipped inside the big tent, right near the front, where they could see all the wonderful things that went on.

Wienerwurst sat pretty quiet on his lap and together they watched the elephants stand on their heads, and the men way up in the air turn somersaults on little swings, and the ladies in bright spangles gallop round and round the ring, and the monkeys and the clowns do tricks - and everything.

Tody was the funniest and happiest of all, and he made all the children laugh and shout and clap their hands. Even Johnny Cricket, the lame boy, who had come a long way to see the circus, smiled.

Marmaduke and Wienerwurst were so excited that they forgot all about Jehosophat and Hepzebiah and the Toyman.

After a while Tody turned a somersault, a cartwheel, and a flipflop, and landed right near their seat.

"How would you like to ride on an elephant?" he whispered in Marmaduke's ear.

Of course Marmaduke answered:

"Better 'n anything I *ever* did."

So Tody took him by the hand and led him into the little tent and put a little pointed cap on his head, just like Tody's own. Then he lifted Marmaduke into a big seat on top of Jumbo, the big elephant. And out they marched under the tent and round and round the ring.

Marmaduke could look down on all the rows of people. He was up quite high and their faces looked small, but he could tell Jehosophat, and Hepzebiah, and Sammy Soapstone, and Sophy, Lizzie Fizzletree, and Fatty Hamm, too. And *there* was the Toyman walking around, looking everywhere for him.

"'Llo, Toyman," he shouted, and the Toyman looked up and saw Marmaduke in his little pointed cap, way up on the back of the big elephant.

The Toyman waved his hand and smiled. I guess he was very glad to find that Marmaduke wasn't lost after all.

But Jehosophat was wishing that *he* had been lost, so that he could have had that fine chance to be part of the circus.

Suddenly there was a chorus of barks. Marmaduke had

forgotten all about Wienerwurst.

He turned around to look for him and leaned back so far that he almost fell flop off the elephant's back. Tody caught him just in time or there *would* have been trouble.

The trick dogs were coming into the circus now. Some of them were walking on their hind legs.

Marmaduke listened.

There were so many different barks! Just as many as there were dogs, - deep or squeaky, smooth or creaky, rough or happy, gruff or snappy, and one that Marmaduke knew the very minute he heard it.

"*Run - run - run - run - runrunrun!*"

Yes, he knew that little voice. He could tell little Wienerwurst's bark anywhere. Somehow it was different from any doggie's in the world. There he was, frisking and scampering and biting at the other dogs' tails, just in fun.

"*Run - run run - run - runrunrun!*"

And that is just what they did, right into the circus ring where the man in the red cap held out big hoops of paper above the dogs' heads.

The first dog jumped through one hoop, and the second dog jumped through another. Then the man in the red cap held up a third hoop bigger than all the rest.

Another dog, a long tall greyhound, got ready to take

his turn, but I guess Wienerwurst decided all-of-a-sudden that *he* wasn't going to be left out. He just gave the tail of that big dog a little nip, and when the big dog turned around to see what was the matter, why Wienerwurst jumped through the hoop all by himself.

So pleased was he that he ran round the ring, looking up at the people in their seats, with his little pink tongue hanging out in delight.

A great doggie was Wienerwurst.

But soon it was all over and the people left their seats, and walked out of the tent to their homes and their suppers.

Tody the Clown just wouldn't let Marmaduke and little Wienerwurst go. He invited them and his brother and sister and the Toyman, too, to have supper in the tent.

At a long table they sat, with Tody, and the big giant, and the little teeny dwarf, and the Lady-with-the-Long-Long-Beard, and the Lady-with-the-Necklace-of-Snakes. But she put the snakes away and Marmaduke wasn't afraid at all.

Tody the Clown sat by his side and kept his plate full and his cup full too. He didn't forget little Wienerwurst either. *He* had a nice big bone all for himself.

But the time came to say "Good-bye," which they did, to one and all of the kind circus people.

Tody the Clown didn't kiss Marmaduke. He just shook hands. Marmaduke was glad of that. He felt like a real man now. For hadn't he been part of a circus and ridden on an elephant! I guess so!

All Tody said to him was:

"Good-bye, pardner, you just keep smiling and make people happy, and you'll be a circus man too, one of these days."

So the Toyman hitched up "old Methuselah," and the three happy children rode home together, falling asleep in the buggy before ever they reached the White-House-with-the-Green-Blinds by the side of the road.

When you visit that place ask Marmaduke to show you the silver button and the big giant's ring. He keeps them still in his little bureau. But the candy was gone, oh, long ago.

NINETEENTH NIGHT

WIENERWURST'S BRAVE BATTLE

Mr. Sun must have known that it was Jehosophat's birthday, he made it so bright, not too sunny nor yet too cool.

The three children, Mother, Father, and the Toyman, were all crowding about something which stood in front of the barn. The three tails of three doggies wagged as if they thought it was fine. Mr. Stuckup came to take a look. So did Miss Crosspatch and the Wyandottes; and the pigeons flew down from their house on the roof and perched on its seat.

It was something for Jehosophat, of course. It was his birthday, and he had tried hard to be good ever since he had had that talk with the tall man on the white horse in the picture.

It was something he had always wanted, - a little cart with a real live pony in the shafts. And the pony all dressed in new harness, spick and span and shiny.

Not very tall was the little pony. His ears twitched just on a level with Jehosophat's head.

Jehosophat put his arm around his neck and patted his

black coat, which was almost as shiny as the harness itself. He looked at the tail. It was nearly a yard long and very thick. That pony was certainly handsome. And Father had given him - cart, harness, and all - to Jehosophat for his birthday, for his very own, to keep just as long as the pony lived. And that was the finest present any boy could have - ever.

The name was a very important matter. The boys each had a dozen they could think of, but Mother and Father and the Toyman couldn't think of any. At least they wouldn't give any suggestions. They thought it was Jehosophat's right to name his own pony.

It was settled at last, - "Little Geeup." Where-ever Jehosophat got that name nobody knew. I really believe he read a story once about a horse called that. Or perhaps he remembered one of the circus ponies with the same name. Anyway, that was the one he chose. So it can't be changed now, any more than Jehosophat's own, or Marmaduke's, or Hepzebiah's.

A moment more they looked Little Geeup all over, from the black mane on his neck down his sleek back to his fine full tail. A moment more they looked at the little cart, its bright red body with the blue lines around it, the wheels and spokes, which were bright yellow, and the shafts and the whiffletrees, which were yellow too.

Then they got in. Little Hepzebiah sat on the seat with Jehosophat. He proudly held the reins. Marmaduke sat behind, his legs hanging over the tail-board, with Wienerwurst wriggling on his lap.

"Tluck, tluck," called Jehosophat. Little Geeup obeyed.

The yellow wheels turned, and down the driveway they went, Father and the Toyman hurrying alongside, Rover and Brownie barking behind.

There were lots of fine carriages out that day, but never so fine a turnout as that little red cart with the yellow wheels and the black pony in the shafts.

Jehosophat didn't have to learn how to drive Little Geeup. Father had often let him drive Old Methuselah when they went to town, and the little black pony was quite safe.

At last Father and the Toyman stopped and waved good-bye. So off the children drove, up the road by the river.

"Where shall we go?" asked Jehosophat.

Now Marmaduke was thinking over something Tody the Clown had told him - about making other folks happy.

"Let's take Johnny Cricket for a ride," he suggested.

The driver agreed, so they turned from the road by the river and drove up a lane. At the end was a house. It was a very small house and a poor one too. Here lived Johnny Cricket, the lame little fellow, who never could run or play like the three happy children.

There wasn't much furniture in his home, or much money either, hardly enough to buy him new crutches, to say nothing of toys that little boys like.

"Whoa!" called Jehosophat, in front of the gate.

Robert Gordon Anderson

Then he got out and knocked at the door.

It opened. Johnny's Mother was there.

Jehosophat took off his hat.

"Good-morning, Mrs. Cricket, can we take Johnny for a ride in my new cart?"

"Of course," replied she. "My! Won't Johnny be glad to go for a ride in that pretty cart! He's been very lonesome."

So out hobbled Johnny, all smiles. Crunch, crunch, crunch went his crutch down the gravel walk.

"Hepzebiah, you'll have to sit in the back with Marmaduke," commanded the owner of the little cart.

So the little girl climbed over the back of the seat and sat with Marmaduke and Wienerwurst. And they helped Johnny in carefully, and off they drove up the lane, enjoying the woods and the nice warm sun. Johnny enjoyed it ever so much, but not more than they. I guess the three children were quite as happy, for to make others happy brings the best sort of happiness.

At last they turned round and drove back.

They were just trotting past the Miller Farm when they heard a great growl.

Over the fields, with great leaps, a big dog was running. Now Jake Miller's dog, Prowler, was the worst dog in the neighbourhood. Often the three children had heard Father say "He ought to be shot."

And there he was - running straight towards them, and little Wienerwurst had jumped over the tailboard and out of the wagon, and was trotting alongside.

"*Urrururur*," growled Prowler. He had almost reached the gate. He was long and big, and really looked more like a savage animal than a dog. Pieces of chain hung from his neck and dragged alongside in the earth as he ran. He must have broken away from his kennel.

Through the gate he bounded, then stopped still and growled in suspicion.

"*Out - out - out*!" he seemed to be saying. He thought they had no right in front of his home, not even when they were driving on the road, which was free to all.

The three happy children and Little Geeup didn't like the looks of things very much.

"Here, Wienerwurst - come here," called Marmaduke. He wanted his little dog to jump back in the wagon and be safe.

But Wienerwurst was no coward. Besides, he was a friendly little fellow, and liked to be polite to everybody, dogs and people too, even if sometimes he did chase the pretty pink pigeons and the White Wyandottes. But that was just in fun, of course.

So he just stood still and looked at the big bad dog and wagged his tail in a friendly way, and smiled.

But that big bad dog Prowler didn't appreciate that at all. He opened his big jaws and showed his teeth and gave a deep growl.

Robert Gordon Anderson

"*Out - out - out!*" he repeated.

And then Wienerwurst gave his tail a wag, and advanced a step or two.

Quick as lightning Prowler jumped at him.

Wienerwurst didn't run. Yet he was so little and the other dog was so big. And his ear hurt too, where the other dog bit him.

The big dog was jumping at him again and again and biting him too, but I guess Wienerwurst must have heard Father and the Toyman tell the boys once never to start a fight, but always to stand up for one's rights, and never to be a coward, or run away.

That Prowler had no right at all to tell him to get off the road nor to bite him!

And so, though he was only a yellow dog and small and weak, Wienerwurst barked bravely and tried his best to fight off the big dog.

It wasn't a very happy chorus of growls and barks and squeals. It sounded something like this:

"*Gurrrrr - gurrr-uh - ow - ow - gurr - gurr - ow - wuf - ar - gurr - ow - wow - uh-wuf - xxx - x!!!*"

Jehosophat pulled on the reins.

"We must stop that," said he. "Hepzebiah you sit here."

Out he jumped, but his brother was ahead of him, for Marmaduke loved Wienerwurst even more than they did.

At the big dog's collar they pulled, and they grabbed tight hold of his chain, trying to drag him away so that he wouldn't hurt little Wienerwurst. But he was very strong, that wicked bad dog. They couldn't budge him at all.

But just then they heard the sound of wheels. They were glad.

Help was coming at last!

A wagon drove up. It was the country postman, who delivered the mail to the farms, in a wagon.

"Whoa!" the postman shouted and out he jumped with his whip!

He ran straight for the big dog, and out of the gate ran Jake Miller too. I guess he felt ashamed of himself for keeping such a dog as Prowler. The two men grabbed the chain and whipped the big bad dog till he let go of Wienerwurst and ran back to his kennel.

Tenderly the two boys lifted their little friend into the cart, and drove home as fast as they could.

They forgot all about the pony and the fine new cart, just thinking of their poor hurt doggie.

Mother and the Toyman brought water in a basin, and the Toyman poured something from a bottle, which coloured the water all dark. With a little clean rag he washed out the cuts on Wienerwurst's face and the back of his neck.

Robert Gordon Anderson

Then out to the workshop he went and brought back a little can. He unscrewed the top and took out some of the salve inside. It was coloured just like peanut-butter and was soft and healing. On each cut he put a little of the salve, then wound the little doggie all up in nice soft bandages too. And Wienerwurst licked the Toyman's hand to show how thankful he was.

They made him a little bed, but he didn't stay in that long. The Toyman was such a good doctor that Wienerwurst felt better already. Still he didn't play very much that day.

Mother sent the Toyman over to the Cricket farm to ask Johnny's mother to let her boy stay for the night.

He did - for *three whole days* - and great fun they had with Little Geeup, and the red dogcart, and the little lame boy, giving Wienerwurst rides to make him all well.

And Father and the Toyman made Jake Miller chain up the wicked dog - very tight this time - with a chain that would never break.

And soon that bad dog died, which was a good thing too. Nobody wasted many tears on him.

But little Wienerwurst got well and strong, and chased the pretty pink pigeons - in fun of course - just as fast as ever he did.

TWENTIETH NIGHT

THE LIONS OF THE NORTH WIND

By the fire sat the Toyman.

He must have been seeing things in the flames, for he kept looking, looking all the time.

He was all alone, for Father and Mother Green had gone to town to see a fine wedding. It was not often that they stayed out so late, but this was a grand event. And they knew the three happy children would be safe in the Toyman's care.

They were all in the next room. Jehosophat and Hepzebiah were sound asleep - but not Marmaduke. He was sitting up, a little bit of a fellow in a big bed.

Outside, old Giant Northwind roared and roared. Now he seemed to be running around and around the house, faster than any train. Now he stopped to knock at the door and bang at the window panes. Now he trampled on the roof, knocking off pieces of slate and a brick from the chimney, which fell, *crash*, through the glass cover of the little greenhouse.

Marmaduke did not like the sounds cruel Giant Northwind made. And it was very dark in the room. To

　　　Robert Gordon Anderson

tell the truth he was just a little bit frightened. But he didn't say anything at all. For the Toyman had told him always to be "game." That was a funny word, but Marmaduke knew what it meant. A brave little boy must not cry even if he *is* afraid.

Still the Giant Northwind kept running round and round the house with great leaps. And the windows creaked, and the trees thumped the house with their branches.

Suppose the Giant should break in and carry him 'way, 'way off!

The door of the next room was open. Through it he could see the bright fire. Higher and higher leaped the flames, as if they wanted to jump up the chimney and join the Northwind in his mad race.

Very comfy and bright looked the fire. Very funny were the shadows on the wall, dancing and bowing to each other and jumping up and down like Jacks-in-the-Box.

One shadow was like a man's, as tall as the ceiling.

Had Giant Northwind gotten in the house at last!

Marmaduke shivered and crept out of bed - and hurried into the next room. He kept as far away from that giant shadow as he could. But he never cried out. He was very brave.

On and on against the wall he tiptoed towards the chair by the fire, where the Toyman sat, thinking his strange thoughts.

The Toyman felt a tug at his sleeve. He looked around. There stood Marmaduke, pointing at the shadow.

That shadow was so big and Marmaduke was so small.

"Don't let him get me!" the little boy cried.

The Toyman reached down and in a second Marmaduke was safe in his arms.

"There's nobody here but me," said the Toyman.

Loud the Giant Northwind howled and roared, while the flames leaped up the chimney.

"Look there!" cried Marmaduke. "There he is!!"

And again he pointed to the shadow on the wall.

"The Giant Northwind has got in our house!"

But the Toyman only laughed, hugging him tighter.

"That's not old Northwind, that's only my shadow," he explained.

Then Marmaduke laughed too.

"Tell me a story, Toyman," he asked, "'bout that ole Giant Northwind."

"It might scare you," the Toyman answered.

Marmaduke only shook his head.

"Nothing makes me scared when I'm *here*," he said.

Robert Gordon Anderson

He wasn't afraid of giants, or ogres, or wild animals, or anything, when he was safe in the Toyman's arms.

For a while he looked up into his face. The Toyman's hair stood up, all funny and rough. He was always running his fingers through it. His face had wrinkles like hard seams, and it was as brown as saddle leather from working outdoors. But Marmaduke thought that nowhere in the world was there so kind a face, except his Mother's.

The Toyman put down his corncob pipe and began:

"Once upon a time, long time ago, before your mother was born, or your grandmother, or your great-grandmother either, there was a King. He was King of all the Winds. And he lived in a great big cave up in a high mountain."

"Was the mountain as high as the church steeple?" asked Marmaduke.

"Oh, higher than that - as high as a lot of church steeples, stuck one on top of another," the Toyman explained.

"Sometimes the King of the Winds took a little snooze in his cave, and then everything was quiet. But when he woke up he would go out of his cave, raisin' ructions all over the world.

"There was a lot of work for him to do, east and west, south and north. He tossed the branches of the trees and made 'em crack, and he made the waves in the ocean turn somersaults, and blew the wooden ships across the sea, and chased the cloud-ships across the sky.

"And he had a lot of little chores too, like drying the clothes on Mondays, and waving the flags on Fourth of July, and sailing little boy's kites high in the air.

"When the King of the Winds was a young fellow, it was all great fun. But after a while the trees grew bigger and bigger, and the ships taller and taller, and there were so many clouds that he got very tired. He was getting pretty old and he ached in all of his bones.

"So he said to himself, said he:

"'I'll let the kiddies do the work, and rest for a spell in my cave on the mountains.'

"There were four of 'em - two boys and two girls - and each had a name, of course. Southwind and Westwind were the girls, Eastwind and Northwind the boys, two strapping big fellows.

"So he called his children together and sat in the door of his cave.

"First he took a big pinch o' snuff. That was a very bad habit folks had in those days.

"*Kerchoo*! he sneezed, and blew two big clouds out of the sky.

"*Kerchoo*!!! he sneezed again, and turned upside down a whole fleet of ships in the ocean.

"*Kerchooooooo*!!!! he sneezed a third time, and blew off the roofs from all the houses in the city, a hundred

Robert Gordon Anderson

miles away.

"When he was all through his sneezing he said to his children:

"'Get ye out to the four corners of the earth and take up my business.'

"Now for a cane the old King used a tree with the branches pulled off. He picked it up and pointed to the south.

"'Southwind, you go there.'

"She was a pretty little thing, with blue eyes and roses in her hair. And she answered him sweet as you please, 'All right, Daddy,' and out she danced.

"Then with the big tree cane, the old King pointed to the west.

"'Westwind, there is your place,' he said.

"A very pretty girl too was Westwind, with kind eyes and a soft smile. Her voice was soft and low, and she answered in a whisper:

"'Good-bye, Daddy dear.'

"She kissed him on the forehead, and floated away to her new home in the west.

"Then the two boys came before the old King. The big tree cane pointed east.

"'Get to work over there, Eastwind,' commanded the

old King.

"Now Eastwind was a strong fellow, but he was surly and cross and he didn't obey very quickly. So his father the King picked up his tree cane in a rage and whacked him across the shins, and out Eastwind ran, crying and yelling till the trees of the forests sobbed too. And he cried so hard that rivers of tears ran from his eyes and over the earth.

"Once more the old King picked up his big tree cane, and said to the eldest of his sons:

"'Northwind, your home is right here in the North.'

"Bigger even than his brother was Northwind. Strong were his muscles, and his whiskers and hair were covered with icicles. When he breathed, millions of snowflakes danced from his mouth.

"*Brrrrrrr*!! how one shivered when he was around.

"Then the old King's hand trembled and the big cane dropped to the floor. He laid him down in the cavern and breathed his last. He had been a great King but he was deader than a doornail now.

"So his four children took up his work.

"Up and down the south country wandered Southwind, with her rosebud mouth and golden hair. And wherever she went she scattered posies and violets upon the earth.

"Back and forth over her country floated Westwind with her soft smile and gentle voice. She whispered lullabies to little children, and laid cool hands on sick people's foreheads. She blew little boy's kites up ever so high above the church steeple, and tried never to break them. And she blew the white ships gently across the ocean. Folks liked to travel the waters whenever she was about.

"But they didn't like Eastwind very much. Sometimes he was all right, but usually he was bent on mischief, making trouble for every man Jack. The seas he would tumble about, turn over the ships, and drown the poor sailors. He would call his grey clouds together and they would weep till the rivers were full. Then he would blow the rivers over the banks, and spoil the gardens, and break the bridges, and drown the poor sheep, and all the rest of the animals too.

"But the most cruel of all was Giant Northwind. Where his heart ought to be was a chunk of ice. Sometimes he was pleasant enough, but most often he was hard and unkind. He would breathe on people, and freeze their noses and toeses, and leave many a poor fellow stiff on the snow.

"Northwind grew and grew till he was the biggest giant on earth. Most as tall as a mountain himself was he, and when he raised his arm he could nearly touch the sky. He kept walking up and down the earth, roaring and hollering fit to blow his lungs out. And how he could travel! He could go clear around the world in about a week.

"One fine day he went out for a walk and he saw Mr. Sun riding up high in the sky. Mr. Sun was a strange sort of a chap, all dressed up in gold armour. The gold armour shone so bright you could never see his eyes or his nose or his mouth, when he walked in the sky.

"Giant Northwind grew very jealous of Mr. Sun. He wanted that fine suit of gold armour, for all he had himself was his long whiskers and his fur coat of snow.

"At Mr. Sun he shook his fist.

"Mr. Sun only laughed at him.

"'Ho, ho!' he said, 'Ho, ho!' and again 'Ho, ho!'

"'Ho, ho! you say,' mimicked Northwind, very angry, 'soon you will laugh on the other side of your mouth. I will blow you out and people can't see your fine suit of gold armour any more.'

"'Ho, ho!' Mr. Sun laughed back. 'Just try it and see. Might as well save your breath.'

"That made Northwind very mad. So he took a deep breath until his chest puffed way out like a big balloon.

"Then he let go. All the hills in the north country shook at that roar.

"And the clouds came hurrying out of the mountains and covered the sky so you couldn't see the Sun and his fine suit at all.

"'Ho, ho!' laughed the Northwind.' Now you will laugh on the other side of your mouth, Mr. Sun.'

"Then he sat him down in his cave to enjoy himself.

"But what was that!

Robert Gordon Anderson

"There was a little hole in the clouds. Through the chink he saw gold shining. Then more and more gold. In a few moments Mr. Sun was riding up in the sky, as big as life.

"'Ho, ho!' said Mr. Sun, 'who laughs last, laughs best.'

"Then old Giant Northwind grew madder and madder, madder than a hornet, yes, just as mad as Mother Wyandotte when Wienerwurst chased her into the brook.

"He took a deep breath, did Giant Northwind, so deep that he almost burst his lungs. He blew and he puffed and he puffed and he blew till the whole sky was filled with grey clouds. And you couldn't see Mr. Sun and his fine suit of gold armour at all.

"Then down he would sit in his cave to enjoy himself for a spell, but by and by, sure as shooting, Mr. Sun would come back again.

"So, for a hundred years, Northwind tried to blow out the Sun. But at last he gave it up as a bad job.

"When he was still a middling young fellow, only about a thousand years old or so, he went walking up and down the earth one night, just after dark.

"He came to a great forest. In it he saw something bright, like a little piece of the Sun. Now he was taller than the tallest tree in the forest, so he got down on his knees to peek between the trunks and see better. People were sitting around the bright little piece of the Sun, and warming their hands, and cooking their supper. Of course it was only a merry fire, but Giant

Northwind was sure it was a piece of the Sun that had fallen on the Earth. He had been so busy trying to blow him out of the sky that he hadn't noticed these little fires much before.

"But he had grown very cross as he knelt there, looking through the trees, and he said to himself, said he:

"'Ho, ho! That's one of the Sun's children. I'll blow that out anyway.'

"And he took a deep breath and puffed his cheeks out.

"*Whurrrooooo*! he breathed on that little piece of the Sun.

"But the little fire just laughed and leaped higher and higher.

"So he took a real deep breath this time, till he filled all his chest, and it stuck way out like the strong man's in the circus.

"*Whurrrrrrooooooooooooooooo*!!!! he roared, but the little flames just danced in the air, as bright and as merry as could be.

"The more he blew the bigger grew the fire, and the sooner the people had their suppers.

"Then for years and years the old Giant stamped up and down the Earth, trying to put out those little pieces of the Sun. And he couldn't do it at all. Like their father, the Sun, the little fires just laughed at him.

Robert Gordon Anderson

"At last Northwind said to himself, said he: "'I know what I'll do, I'll get me some big grey wolves to put out those fires.'

"So a-hunting he went, up into the biggest forests of the world, so dark that people called them 'the Forests of Night.' And they were full of fierce grey wolves.

"With his strong hands he caught a hundred wolves and drove them back to his cave.

"Then one dark night when the people were sitting around their fires, so cozy and nice, he untied the wolves and roared out:

"'Wolves, put out those fires!'

"And the fierce grey wolves ran out of the cavern, and snapped and snarled at the little fires. But they couldn't put them out. So back they came to the cave, with their tongues hanging out and their tails between their legs.

"'Good-for-nothings,' roared Northwind, 'I'll get me some tigers.'

"Again he went stalking over the Earth till he reached the great deserts, which the people called 'the Deserts Without End.' Here he caught a thousand fierce tigers and drove them back to his cave.

"The next night, while the people were talking and singing around the little fires, he let the tigers loose.

"'Tigers,' roared he, 'put out those fires.'

"They ran out of the cave, making a terrible noise, and

they raced up and down the earth, with their sharp teeth gleaming, and their tails lashing. At the fires they snarled, and growled, and roared, and tried to beat out the flames with their paws. But they were only burned for their trouble. And so the tigers too slunk back to the cave, with their heads hanging down and their tails between their legs.

"Once more the Northwind stalked forth and hunted through the highest mountains he could find, so high that people called them 'the Roof of the World.' Ten thousand lions he caught, the fiercest in all the Earth. He tied them together by their tails, ten at a time, and drove them back to his cave.

"And he sent them out too.

"'Lions, put out those fires!'

"Such a terrible roar those lions roared that the whole Earth shook. Through the forests they raced, leaping through the wild tree tops, lashing their tails, and shaking their shaggy manes. And they leaped at the fires, but they couldn't do any better. Those big lions just couldn't put the little fires out.

"Beside himself with rage was old Northwind now. So he sent them all out, wolves and tigers and lions wild, and he rushed on at their head.

"But never, never can they put the little fires out, so you needn't worry at all."

The Toyman stopped and Marmaduke listened.

"Hark!"

Yes, there were the grey wolves now, howling down the chimney. There were the wild tigers, snarling at the window panes and leaping at the door.

Hark! How the knobs rattled!

And there were the wild lions, rushing and roaring through the tree-tops.

And round and round and round the house raced old Giant Northwind himself.

But all the while, in the fireplace the little red flames danced merrily, never afraid at all.

Marmaduke jumped. Something was whining and scratching at the door.

Was it a wolf?

The voice he heard was too small and weak.

He knew who *that* was.

"Toyman," he shouted, "that's my little pet doggie, out in the cold. Those bad wolves an' tigers an' lions 'll eat him up."

So they ran to the door, the Toyman and little Marmaduke. And he wasn't afraid at all. And they let little Wienerwurst in, and saved him from the grey wolves and the wild tigers and the fierce lions of the Northwind.

Little Wienerwurst barked happily and curled himself up by their feet, in front of the warm fire.

After that Marmaduke spoke only once before he fell asleep.

"You never had any little boys, did you, Toyman?"

On the Toyman's face was a funny look as he answered:

"No, little feller, I never had any little boys."

Marmaduke reached up his hand and patted the Toyman's rough, kind face.

"Don't worry, Toyman," he said, "*I'll* be your little boy."

Little Wienerwurst was sound asleep, so Marmaduke just had to fall asleep too, happy and safe in the Toyman's arms, by the little red fire that the wind could never put out.

Robert Gordon Anderson